A TALE OF TWO MIGRATIONS

A FRENCH CANADIAN ODYSSEY

by Patrice Demers Kaneda

DENVER, COLORADO

Outskirts Press, Inc.
http://www.outskirtspress.com

ISBN: 978-1-4787-1336-4

Outskirts Press and the "OP" logo are trademarks belonging to Outskirts Press, Inc.

To Kunihiro my husband who made the book possible with his patience, technical skills and the drives along the King's Highway.

And for my children, grandchildren and great grandchildren so they will know our beginnings.

Warm thanks to my granddaughter, Anna Duprey, for her research and interest, and to my dear friends Catherine Kalonia and Tricia Dupont for the hours they gave so willingly, to Margery Nichols for her painstaking editing, to Jacques and Sylvia Navarro for their hospitality during our treks through Normandy, and to Doris Hoser for making our trip to Erlangen happen with her wonderful friends, Doris and Klaus Ruppert.

With humble thanks to my friends in The Writing Group at the Osher Lifelong Learning Institute of Northwestern University for their help and encouragement over these many years.

Finally, this book is dedicated to those who are gone but not forgotten, my artist friend, Ethel Peterson, my memeres, Rhea and Elizabeth, my wonderful parents, Teddy and Estelle, and Uncle Edouard who brought us to America when he moved to Woodstock Hill.

--Pat Demers Kaneda

Contents

BOOK 2
LA GUERRE DE LA CONQUEST
THE WAR OF THE CONQUEST

BOOK 3
THE SECOND MIGRATION

AUTHOR'S FAMILY NAMES

PATERNAL SIDE	MATERNAL SIDE
DUMAYS-DUMOYS- DIT	
DUMETS-DEMERS	
	GREGOIRE
MAUGIS	BELANGER
	MENARD DIT DURBOIS
CHEF-DE-VILLE	ROUTHIER
PAPIN	RIVARD
GAUTHEIR	CASAUBON
BONIN	AUREZ-LAFERRIERE
BARIL	BOUCHER
DESROSIERS	GERVAIS
LANGEVIN	

PROLOGUE

Southbridge, Massachusetts: My Little Canada

I WAS ALMOST born in Vienna, but the founders reconsidered and named the town Southbridge. The only remnants of the name, Vienna, are a Bed and Breakfast and a German restaurant.

Southbridge, Massachusetts was incorporated on February 15, 1816. It soon attracted a large population, for this was the age of mills. The Quinebaug River ran through the center, providing waterpower. The landscape was beautiful, with rolling hills, excellent forests and rich soil. Its mills served as a magnet to draw Quebecois to the area during the great migration.

Between 1840 and 1930 over 530,000 descendants of the original ten thousand founders of *Nouvelle-France* traveled to New England in search of better lives. They were the *Canadiens*, the *Quebecois*. Around the same time, eight million immigrants flowed into New York City to escape the poverty of Europe. We know of their passage through Ellis Island but fewer know of those Canadians who walked, came by horseback, or by train and made their way to Maine, New Hampshire, Massachusetts, Connecticut , Vermont and Rhode Island--- to a new life.

Southbridge became one of several "Little Canadas" that sprang up in New England in the late 1800s. Over sixty percent of its population was Quebecois.

I was born in 1935 and spent the first thirteen years of my life in Southbridge. From the age of six, I attended *Notre Dame Academie Brochu*, the school founded by the Parish of Notre Dame. Our teachers were Sisters of the Assumption, many of whom came from Canada. We were taught in both French and English and our studies included religion, the history of the United States and French Canada, as well as the usual subjects demanded by the town's curriculum. English studies were in the afternoon. On the playground, speaking French was mandatory. Representatives from the Catholic Diocese of Worcester tested us quarterly in all subjects. Our day was extended during Lent, and in May, the month of Mary, October, the month of Joseph and during other religious holidays when my friends and I would walk to church after supper for evening services.

In 1953, I left my Little Canada forever and gave it up to become American, but it remained in my heart.

Throughout the years I heard bits and pieces about my ancestors. Two Jesuit relatives had done our family genealogy. I thought about the *Quebecois*, and pondered the questions: "But why did they come to Canada and what were their lives like before?"

I delved into history books and took several trips to Paris, Normandy and Quebec and decided to tell their story, not as straight history, but rather as a combination of history, fiction and memoir to bring vibrancy to these people who made two migrations.

THE FIRST MIGRATION

Before the last ice age, some 10,000 years ago, England and France were linked by a chalk landmass. Glaciers broke through it separating England from Europe.

On the English side of the strait that divided them are the White Cliffs of Dover, and on the French side are the *Falaise*, the white cliffs of Normandy. Along that beautiful coast of upper Normandy is the city of Dieppe. If you are one of the millions of people who are descended from the original ten thousand French settlers of Quebec, Canada, it is quite likely that your ancestors are from this area.

In the 16th century when France was one of the most powerful nations on earth, it was a time of exploration and the Port of Dieppe was the point of departure for the sailing ships. It was a city of fishermen, seafaring men, and skilled artisans many of whom were ivory carvers. Sadly, it was also a center of the slave trade.

Overlooking the city and its harbor then and now is a magnificent chateau that survived the Dutch and English bombardment at the end of the XV11 century.

If you are one of the over five million descendants of those original ten thousand who settled Quebec and called themselves *Canadiens*, this may be your story. For others, it's a little known piece of the American mosaic.

A HISTORICAL NOTE

SAMUEL DE CHAMPLAIN, FOUNDER OF QUEBEC, 1608

THE YEAR 2008 marked the four hundredth anniversary of the founding of Quebec. There would be no story to tell had it not been for the gallant adventurer, Samuel Champlain, and his supporter, the King of France, Henry IV.

Beyond their search for business enterprises, both of these men were humanists who hoped to establish a colony in Quebec where Catholics, Protestants and indigenous people could live in peace and harmony. Both men were converts from Protestantism to Catholicism and had experienced the religious wars that killed millions in Europe within four decades. The King was thought to have said,

"A mass isn't a great price to pay for Paris."

In 1598, he signed the Edict of Nantes that protected the citizens of France from religious persecution. The principal text included ninety-two articles and fifty-six secret articles dealing with Protestant rights and obligations. The Protestants were still obliged to pay tithes and observe Catholic holy days, but they were protected when traveling abroad in the days of the Inquisition and allowed to practice their religion at home.

In France, a country where the Catholic Church kept detailed records of births, marriages and deaths, and where to this day it is relatively simple to find family records going back to 1500, no exact record of Champlain's birth exists. The names of his parents are known, and of his home in Brouage, the first European place for trading salt on France's Atlantic coast, but the range of possible birth dates for him spans ten years. Church records may have been destroyed in the religious wars.

There is speculation by some historians regarding his bond with King Henry. (Champlain received an annual pension from an early age and had access to the King beyond that of others of his class). They posit that he may have been the King's illegitimate son. Some of the speculation comes from an entry in one of Champlain's own books, *Les Voyages* which he wrote in 1632 where he states "...of myself to take the liberty of going on this voyage I could not do so, but by the command of said Majesty, to whom I was under an obligation both by birth and by a pension with which he honoured me as a means to maintain me near him."

The King, called the King of Hearts by his subjects, was known for his virility, and had many illegitimate children. Though there has been much conjecture, no hard proof exists that he was Champlain's father.

What we do know of Samuel Champlain exists in the books that he wrote, and the diaries of those who knew him. His maps and his drawings remain, including some self- portraits. Like Kings before him, his signature was a bold simple, 'Champlain' and so he is known.

We have the dedicated works of many historians who studied and continue to study the life of this great and gifted man, the founder of New France.

Champlain died on Christmas day in 1635.

THE FIRST MIGRATION
BOOK 1

CHAPTER 1
FRANCE TO CANADA

DIEPPE, NORMANDY
Autumn, 1642

Jean Demers hurried from Dieppe Harbor to his home on *La Grande Rue*. He looked back at his ship, *L'Esperance* and thought it wouldn't be long before they would set sail again. He'd been the ship's carpenter for over thirty years, but never tired of the sea.

His wife, Barbe, had no idea of his return for no letters had reached her.

He'd been away for eighteen months and had much to tell the family about his voyage to *Nouvelle-France*. More than that, he had a plan that he hoped they would find agreeable.

He shifted his duffel bag from shoulder to shoulder and only nodded to the merchants who shouted out greetings as he passed their shops. He was a sturdy man and fit for his fifty years. His shock of dark hair was the envy of the crew, and maintenance of the hull, masts and yards had molded his body and muscles into the physique of a much younger man. He would prove his virility tonight when he bedded Barbe. Though she was seven years older, the sight of her still warmed his blood. His pace quickened.

After passing the Huguenots' ivory shops he came to his two-story house at the end of the street. The first floor was on ground level and the second floor opened onto the hill behind it. He pushed open the heavy carved door with a brass knob for it was slightly ajar.

The first to greet him was his daughter, Mary Margaret. He realized that his sons Andre, Etienne and Jean would still be at work on the fishing boats. She ran to him and kissed him on both cheeks. "Papa! It's been so long! Are you well? You look tired. Put down your sack and sit here. I'll get you some drink." She reached for the calvados, but he said,

"I prefer whatever is in that pot over the fire. Where is your mother?"

"She went to carry lunch to the boys down at the harbor. It's a wonder you didn't meet them. They must have seen your ship."

"And Laurent?" he asked, referring to his youngest child.

"He's at the church for catechism."

Between spoonfuls of stew and chunks of bread he spoke. "It's no wonder she missed the ship. There's so much going on there right now. Several large trading ships have come in. We're moored between them. You wouldn't believe the commotion with all the un-loading that's going on. The last ship that came in just ahead of us had a full load of elephant ivory. That captain must be counting on a fortune."

Watching her father sop up the remaining drops of stew with his bread, Mary Margaret quickly took the bowl from him and refilled it.

"Were there many surgeries to perform on this voyage?" This topic was always of interest to her. She marveled at her father's skill after hearing stories from his shipmates whose lives he had saved. Though he'd had no training, early on he had shown a talent for setting bones and performing amputations in emergencies on shipboard, and he was respected as much as a surgeon as he was a carpenter in this city.

"Two legs and an arm, I'm afraid. Young men they were too. In every case we had no choice, for gangrene was setting in. It took strong men to hold them steady and lots of brandy. I kept my tools as sharp as possible for the job to spare them pain. I got it done pretty quickly. They won't be off to sea again, I'm afraid. Though I've seen my share of peg leg sailors, there's less work for those who've lost an arm. Mending nets is all they're good for."

He concentrated on his stew after that, and by the time his Barbe walked through the door he had nodded off. She took a coverlet from the back of a chair and placed it over his lap.

"Your father is glad to be home. He's sleeping off the loneliness."

She'd seen his ship and had stopped to pick up two rabbits and a chicken.

She went about her chores and prepared a special dinner.

A few hours later, the whole family gathered around the rough plank table. After the meal, all eyes were turned toward Jean as they waited to hear his news of *Nouvelle-France*.

He wiped his mouth on his sleeve and looked around the table slowly, until his gaze reached Barbe who was listening intently. He would have to phrase his thoughts carefully. He looked down at his hands.

"There are unlimited opportunities in the new land. You can't imagine the beaver, and lumber--great trees such as you've never seen reaching up into the heavens. It's beautiful country just waiting to be developed and the chance for trade is limitless.

Turning his eyes toward Barbe once again, he continued with caution, for he knew how she felt about her boys. "On my next trip, I'd like our sons to join me. Laurent and Mary Margaret will stay."

His youngest son, only ten, gazed at his mother.

The look on his wife's face made Jean think that he should have waited a little longer to mention his plan. Instead, he turned to his sons.

"Come with me when next we sail and see for yourselves. With your carpentry skills you could be useful on the ship and when we reach land you'll be in great demand. *L'Esperance* will be leaving again in August. What do you say, boys?"

Before they could say a word it was Barbe who spoke up. "All three? You would take three of my sons from me? How could you? Dieppe is thriving. We have all the trade we need right here. Ships are sailing in from Africa every week." She hardly paused for breath.

"The boys have unlimited opportunities here and I had hoped they would study navigation. Our school is the best in Europe and our harbor the busiest in France. They can find plenty of adventure right here."

Jean lowered his voice and reached for Barbe's hand. "I never said they'd have to remain there. I just want them to have the choice and to see for themselves. If they did choose to stay, we could all resettle there. By that time, Laurent could have studied navigation."

At this point, Barbe rose from her chair and rushed outside. The conversation was over.

Dieppe was indeed prosperous. It was the center of the ivory and slave trade. The carvers were highly skilled and their goods were in great demand. Their shops lined the streets. The food stalls were open every day and the women enjoyed the sociability of their daily marketing. Now, a few shoppers seeking bargains awaited this final hour to buy the last of the fish and enough vegetables for a humble soup.

Barbe walked among them just minutes from her door and turned toward the wharf. The tide was in and she stood there, staring at the gray waters pounding on the shore. Above the din, she tried to imagine her life without her sons. Etienne was the eldest, the child of Jean's first marriage to Miotte.

She was a dear friend who died when Etienne was only two. He was now eighteen and as precious to her as the children to whom she gave birth; next was Andre, two years younger, Jean, just fourteen- -each son born nine months after their father's return from a voyage, and finally Laurent. She turned back toward their house now, seeing it almost empty in her mind with only Mary Margaret and little Laurent. There had been many miscarriages and one stillborn child and no hope for more.

Mary Margaret, her first-born, was nearing twenty but she would marry soon. And how Laurent would miss his brothers!

Later that night with the fire banked and the linen panels closed around them, they lay in the large bed that Jean had built for them the first year of their marriage. He spoke to her softly.

"Barbe, you're right that Dieppe is prosperous and we have a good life, but if they stay here they will always be carpenters. They'll never rise beyond their station. In *Nouvelle-France* there's every opportunity. They can be whatever they want to be."

"Grandchildren will be my wealth. I need nothing more. All that I want is right here. The final decision will be theirs, but I don't know if I can bear their leaving."

Letting Barbe have the last word, he refrained from telling her of all the questions the boys had asked when she'd left the house, and of their excitement.

In August, 1643, *L'Esperance* sailed into the harbor of Quebec where Champlain had established a settlement just thirty-five years before. With Jean were Etienne, Andre and Jean Joseph. Barbe would never see her three sons again.

Jean bought eight acres of land along the banks of the St. Laurence River. He worked for a company in France that wanted to establish holdings in Quebec. He was under contract until 1650. He remained the ship's carpenter for a time, and carried news between countries. His trips home were often a year or more apart. When on leave in Dieppe between sailings, Barbe didn't cease reminding him of how empty her home was and of how she missed her sons.

"They're doing well. They're building a beautiful cathedral. Their skills are needed and soon they will take wives. What more do you want, woman?"

He knew the answer. He looked at his son, Laurent, who was now receiving all of his mother's attention and knew that he would never join his brothers.

Mary Margaret helped with the chores and seemed morose. She certainly didn't seem interested in finding a husband. She ignored any suggestions made by her parents about who would be a good match.

Her mother attributed her loneliness to the absence of her three brothers, but she had a secret of her own. She had met a young man when she'd gone to the glove factory. He worked at the front counter where she was fitted for new gloves. He was tall and attentive and had run after her when she'd left her old pair in his shop. After that, they met several times down at the harbor, walking independently and looking straight ahead as they spoke, for he was a *Huguenot*, a word that carried terrible connotations even for her. Neither of them had expected this attraction and realized the family quarrels that would result. Such a bond could only cause distress. But yet, the attraction was there, and they continued to meet.

One afternoon, as Laurent was walking back from catechism class, he saw his sister seated on a large rock with a young man. That evening at supper, he brought up the subject. "Who was that man that you were talking with today? You looked pretty friendly." Mary Margaret felt the blood rising from her neck up to her cheeks. "What man? I was doing an errand down near the harbor and I stopped to rest."

"I saw you, Mary Margaret, and you were talking with him."

"Oh. I might have commented on the weather."

By this time, her mother was noticing her blush and watching as the young woman clasped her hands over and over again in a nervous manner, a sure sign that she wasn't quite comfortable with the conversation.

"Leave your sister alone, Laurent. If she has something to tell us, I'm sure she will do so."

Catholic and Protestant neighbors, seeing them together, began to pay attention and soon both sets of parents heard the news, not from their children, but from others, and there were accusations on both sides.

These were people who were accustomed to living together peacefully under the *Edict* of *Nantes* signed almost fifty years before, which ended the religious wars. Doing commerce, passing the time of day--but marriage? Impossible!

There were laws in place that protected this minority that numbered over two hundred thousand who had converted to the Protestant religion, but their criticism of Catholic doctrine and worship did not set well with the devotees. Above all, the Calvinist criticism of their Holy Father and their accusations that the Papacy was like a monarchy truly drew contention. The word *Huguenot* was used to deride them; even though no one knew the origin of this strange word, it was applied to the French Calvinists by their critics for over a century.

Champlain and King Henry IV had been Calvinists who converted to Catholicism, but some suspected that the King converted just to regain power of Catholic Paris. Had he not said, "Paris is worth a Mass"?

It was Mary Margaret who left her church and her home and became a Protestant.

Before leaving, she'd argued, "Alexandre Langevin is a good man, *Maman*, and his parents are kind people."

Like most Calvinists, his family was middle class and prosperous. Many were skilled artisans. At first, Barbe vowed that she'd never visit Mary Margaret's Protestant home, but when she met her daughter on the street while marketing, and saw that she was pregnant, the thought of grandchildren, even little heathens, was too much to resist. There would be six little ones and in time, there was merriment in Barbe's home when the family came to visit and the shadows were chased from every corner.

Life in Dieppe became more peaceful for Jean, but when he carried the news of his daughter's marriage back to Quebec it was met with shock. *Nouvelle-France* where only Catholics were allowed to immigrate was even less tolerant than France. Their sister a *Huguenot*!

Nouvelle-France, the future capital of a great empire with its hard-working men, natural resources, and nothing more superb than the approach to Quebec on the St. Lawrence River, but where are the women?

CHAPTER 2
PARIS,
TWO DECADES LATER

Thursday, April 16, 1662
Paris, France

The Diary of Catherine Menard

Papa died today. This is the worst day of my life. The doctor came in the afternoon and gave Papa a dose of digitalis for his weakness. After that, he decided to breathe a vein as he'd done on previous days. Then he washed his instruments in the basin of soapy water. After packing his bag, he left, saying that Papa should feel better after a short rest and that he had to stop at a neighbor's to check on a sick child.

Father looked frail lying under the blue wool coverlet. *Maman* tried to feed him some broth, but he was too weak to raise his head. She raised him slightly and gave him a few spoonfuls that just ran down his chin. His breathing was labored and his eyes were closed. He didn't respond to *Maman's* words.

She screamed for me to run for the doctor, but I was frozen in place, just looking down at him. Gripping my arm, Maman said the doctor could not be far off, and again she shouted for me to run.

As my feet pounded the rough cobblestones, I realized that I wasn't wearing shoes. I kept to the side avoiding the garbage and fetid piles of waste in the center of the street. I turned the corner just as the doctor was climbing into a carriage. Slipping in the mud of that unpaved street, I grabbed his hand. Through my tears, I shouted, "Papa is unconscious. Something is terribly wrong. I beg you to come."

When we reached the house, *Maman* and my sisters were staring down at Papa. Yvette, poor little one was stroking his cheek and calling to him to wake up. Marie was staring into his stony face. The doctor examined him.

"His pulse is very weak. I don't know why he took such a turn. This is the end I'm afraid. You'd better call the priest." He spoke those words solemnly with his hand on dear *Maman's* shoulder.

How could this be? Just months ago, our dear Papa was strong and cheerful. He was the dearest man anyone could know. In my mind's eye, I see him behind his bench wearing his leather apron with his tools neatly arranged before him, discussing the latest news with his patrons, and later telling stories as we sat around the long table eating supper by the last light of day.

With his elbows on the table, he would laugh so much while telling a funny story, that it was hard for him to speak. His blue eyes shone and he'd brush his dark curls away from his face. We three listened from the loft each night while he and *Maman* wrote in the receipt book and were lulled by their voices as they discussed the events of the day. And now?

It was I who went to fetch the priest. *Maman* rested her head on Papa's chest for many hours, listening to his labored breathing. The priest performed the sacrament of extreme unction using holy oils. We all prayed.

After receiving the last rites, the end came. It was just before midnight. I am writing this by the light of the full moon, in disbelief, while my sisters, who cried themselves to sleep are in deep slumber at last.

FRIDAY

It was my seventeenth birthday today, but no one remembered. A soft breeze came through the front door when I opened it this morning and birds sang, but I felt no warmth--only icy sorrow as I slipped on my shoes and walked down the street to call on Papa's customers with the sad news. I left *Maman* to arrange the funeral mass.

CHAPTER 3
HOPE-1664

It had been two years since the death of Catherine's father. Jean Claude, his apprentice, had gone to seek another master, for working alone, he had already fallen behind on the orders during Papa's illness. Only Papa could make the new, beautiful shoes, some that were meant for the Royal Court. Dust covered the benches.

Uncle Charles, her mother's brother, helped as much as he could. He had six children of his own and any time that he gave money to his sister, he avoided his wife's watchful eye. There was food for them all, though their stores were dwindling, and there was the problem of the dowries.

Catherine was nineteen and still unmarried. She thought of becoming a nun, for that required a lesser dowry and she would have access to books in the convent. But marriage was the only way that she could help her sisters and her mother. She considered these things as she managed all the household affairs, bartered with food merchants, did mending and knitting, and worked in the early morning hours in her uncle's bakery beside *Maman*.

Catherine and her mother were determined to keep the younger girls in school as long as possible. They too would need dowries and uncle's help could not extend that far. Everyone in her family knew how to read and write and the only hope of continuing their education came from the church.

One spring evening as she walked to deliver some mending to the blind widow Aucoin, Catherine noticed posters nailed to trees along the path. A group of young women were gathered at the entrance to the park and were chatting excitedly as a tall, thin, red-headed girl read aloud:

WANTED BY REQUEST OF KING LOUIE IV
DAUGHTERS OF THE KING
ONE THOUSAND STRONG WOMEN
OF MARRIAGEABLE AGE: 14 TO 40
TO GO TO NEW FRANCE AS BRIDES
THE FOLLOWING WILL BE ACCEPTED
ORPHANS AND WIDOWS,
A GIRL ACCOMPANIED BY ONE PARENT
NO GIRL GOING TO JOIN A FIANCE OR HUSBAND
WILL BE ACCEPTED
UPON THE SIGNING OF A MARRIAGE CONTRACT
IN NEW FRANCE A DOWRY WILL BE PRESENTED
ALONG WITH A SUM OF UP TO 200 FRANCS
IF YOU ARE OF GOOD HEALTH AND GOOD MORALS
GO TO THE KING'S AGENT AT CITY HALL

Catherine's thoughts turned to her Papa who had spoken many times about New France. The newspaper articles were often critical of the millions of francs that were going to develop that vast land and of the many men that had been sent on contract from Normandy to bring back furs and start colonization.

His words came back to her. Leaning back in his chair, pipe in hand; he was discussing the British settlement of Plymouth. "If they had just come to our Paris bookshops in 1613, they could have bought Champlain's book, *Voyage de Nouvelle-France*. There, they would have found maps of an area he'd named Port St-Louis, which they named Plymouth. He should have left the French flag there to greet them."

She recalled that Papa told the whole history of *La Nouvelle-France* beginning with the story of a group called Adventurers of England who controlled the fur trade around Hudson Bay where tribes, and particularly the Iroquois, brought their furs every spring to trade for knives, kettles, beads, needles and blankets.

The Adventurers became rich trying to satisfy the insatiable appetite of our country and theirs for beaver hats. That animal had become extinct in Europe and nothing compared to it in quality. Its fur was waterproof and warm.

Papa would get excited when he'd talk about how powerful France was.

"France tried for a hundred years to have a settlement in North America. Were we not the most powerful nation on earth? Our army under Louis IV numbered nearly a half million. No army since the Romans had such resources for colonizing and conquering new lands."

In Florida, French Huguenots established a small colony in 1564 that was later sacked by the Spanish Catholics before they settled St. Augustine. There was no chance of them living peacefully with Protestant Huguenots. The Spanish slaughtered every one. France's old enemies, the British, continued to wage war. They had settlements south of what later became Quebec and Montreal and they wanted more of the trade. Their settlements on the east coast of America far outnumbered those of France.

In the New World, Samuel Champlain established a colony in a place the Mohawks called *Kebec*, meaning the place where the great river narrows. He had sailed from the harbor of Honfleur with its history of slave trade, with Captain Gregoire in charge of his ship. It was 1608, and there were several hundred French Catholic settlers. Huguenots, Calvinist Protestants, were excluded after the Edict of Nantes was revoked.

In 1640, the King encouraged investors to form the Company of One Hundred Associates. The associates were granted land and created *seigneuries*, feudal land holdings in Quebec that could be subdivided and ceded to qualified immigrants.

The hundreds of new settlers that signed on between 1640 and 1650 kept the small colony from extinction, but even now, more than four decades later, there were only thirty-two hundred inhabitants.

Many of the men who signed on came from the Perche region of Normandy, about one hundred miles west of Paris. They were called "Thirty-six Monthers," for that was the length of their contracts. Most were bachelors over thirty, looking for change and opportunities beyond their humble status. In a few year's time, Normandy was doing well in the lumber and fur business. The men from Perche were paid from forty to one hundred twenty francs a year in addition to receiving some land.

They were mostly illiterate, could usually sign their names, and came from all trades. They were fur merchants, lumbermen, domestics, laborers, masons, gunsmiths, woodworkers, master knife sharpeners, laundrymen, hatters, and master tailors. Some received shoes, cloaks and a small advance on their salary. Very few sailed with wives and children. Women who went alone numbered less than ten each year, and earned meager wages. More women were desperately needed for the growth of the colony.

Catherine remembered more of her father's stories. He'd told the family how a few years after the founding of Quebec, at the age of fifty-two, Mr. Champlain himself had returned to France for a bride. Helene Eustache de Bouille was betrothed to him. She was twelve. They were married on December 27th, 1610. Everyone was happy about the match, for Champlain and her father had known each other for years. Everyone, that is, except the headstrong girl who'd been forced to marry against her will.

He returned to New France without her, but with a generous dowry of four thousand five hundred francs for the new settlement. Helene's father was a highly placed finance minister to the King.

The reluctant bride joined Samuel four years later when she was sixteen. Her husband was appointed governor in 1620.

In Paris, people knew of this woman's courage. Her diaries and those of nuns who'd lived in Quebec were widely read. Helene stayed there for just four years, and was admired and respected by the settlers and by the Indians whom she taught.

After her husband's death in 1635, Helene entered the convent of Ursuline Sisters that she had founded earlier, and stayed in France for the rest of her life.

Maman had said, "Imagine Helene's arrival in the new land after her life of comfort and elegance as the daughter of a Duke who was Secretary to the King. After the glory of Versailles, what must she have thought when she saw a few rough dwellings and teepees in a land of rock, water and forests? She had three servants in attendance who carried her fine clothes and books. Was she prepared to step in mud with her elegant little slippers? Perhaps they carried her! Was she prepared to take her place as the bride of an old man?"

After talking with *Maman* and her sisters, filled with resolve, Catherine gathered the necessary documents, her birth certificate and a statement from a priest stating that she was eligible to marry.

"If Helene could give up her life in France to help the new colony, perhaps I can do it for my family. I will pray to the *Bon Dieu* to give me courage."

CHAPTER 4

ANDRE: A SPECIAL FRIEND

For days, the possibility of taking the journey was on Catherine's mind. But another memory, one tinged with sadness, entered her mind. She remembered Andre, her friend who'd gone to Nouvelle-France the winter before her father died in 1649. Somehow, memories of her father's death and Andre's absence melded in her mind leaving her with a feeling of emptiness.

She remembered Andre's clear brown eyes and his soft voice as he'd helped her up that winter day when they'd skated together on the beautiful River Seine. Surprised to see him before her, she'd scrambled up, clinging to his good arm, hoping that he hadn't noticed her torn hose as she pulled down her long woolen skirt. Moments later, she'd had to help him up and they'd laughed about that.

She'd known him for many years as a cheerful boy in her neighborhood. Sometimes, he would follow her home from school or church and tease her about her curly black hair or her very straight posture, but she knew it was meant kindly. If he happened to meet her mother on the street, he'd offer to help her carry her baskets from the market. He'd come right into their small house and barely glance at Catherine. But she felt his sidelong look as he prepared to leave holding a thick slice of bread and butter that *Maman* insisted that he take.

When she met him before her father's death more than a year ago, Andre, now a soldier, was on leave for a few days before departing once more. He was a member of the *Carignan-Salieres* Regiment. Just months before, together with Austrian and German troops, he'd been in a fierce battle against the Turks and had suffered a saber wound to his shoulder.

The day they'd met on the frozen river was the first day she'd seen him out of the uniform in which he'd taken so much pride during their last meetings, for it was the very first uniform for the regiment. The brown, well-tailored jacket and trousers with gray facings suited him, but the tall hat rather resembled that of a bishop's miter, causing her to smile inwardly at his expense.

She liked him better the way she saw him this day in his colorful knitted hat and his pantaloons. He looked like any other young man, but she'd heard from Papa about the horrors that this regiment had experienced fighting the Turks. So many young boys had died in battle or later of their wounds.

Andre was lucky, though his injured shoulder left him with a permanent shrug on one side. Her heart beat faster at the sight of him, and she felt a smile that came with a blush. That hadn't happened when they were children.

Before Papa's illness, when a dowry had seemed possible, Andre had been very much on her mind, but would she have had the courage to follow him to the New World? Would he always remain a soldier? His regiment of twelve hundred men was going there because of the fear of Indian uprisings. The Iroquois sided with the British against the Hurons and the Algonquins and the French. Recently, they had won some battles.

King Louis was determined to protect his investment in the small colony, especially since there was an agreement between the French and the Hurons that the French would be allies against their enemies, the Iroquois. This alliance kept the Iroquois out of the fur trade.

Catherine had seen Andre march away with others after a brief goodbye. She remembered his words during their last meeting. Dear Papa had been present that day and Andre had spoken honestly. "When I left to fight the Turks I felt so strong, so brave. My friends and I joked about how we'd wipe them out, but the reality of it was quite another thing. To face the Turks with their sabers and to see limbs fly through the air and the ground wet with the blood of young men from both sides is something I'll never forget. Now, we are going to fight warriors who have proven their strength time and time again. Their numbers are great and we don't know their style of combat. We'll soon learn I'm afraid. Somehow, I feel less confident and only hope to return to France as soon as we establish peace. Our Governor, Mr. Champlain, is hoping to sign some treaties soon."

Papa shook his hand vigorously and the two men hugged.

"God bless you and keep you safe." Papa said. Catherine spoke the same words quietly in her mind.

The men had left the pikes behind that they'd used in combat with the Turks. They would be of no use against the fighting style of the Iroquois who used ambush tactics from behind trees and rocks. Instead, the soldiers were issued matchlock and flintlock muskets with bayonets. They all carried swords.

Little did Catherine know that marriage was probably the farthest thing from Andre's thoughts when he arrived in Nouvelle-France on the 17th of June, 1665.

After a difficult journey, where they'd experienced rough seas and rancid food, the soldiers disembarked. They were met by cheering crowds of their countrymen and Indians who'd suffered greatly from random attacks by Iroquois warriors. In addition, diseases brought by the Jesuits who had come to save their souls had already decimated the native people. In a village that had contained over ten thousand people, there remained but a thousand. Knowing that the survivors were greatly weakened, the Iroquois had chosen this opportunity to destroy *Huronia*, the village of the Hurons, once and for all. They killed as many people as they could as they attempted to flee, including the Jesuit priests who lived among them.

With orders from the King, the *Carignan* soldiers were divided into two groups: one that would remain in the settlement and the other who marched off in search of these enemies. Andre was among the five hundred French soldiers who marched into the wilderness.

The *Carignan* soldiers were unfamiliar with the climate, the distances and the fighting tactics of these warriors that they hoped to meet. Poorly dressed, each one had just one pair of shoes and a blanket. Winter came early in Nouvelle-France and ships carrying clothes, supplies, weapons and money to pay the soldiers would not arrive until spring.

They trudged through forests for weeks, not meeting the enemy and, without realizing it, they'd reached western New York and wandered into a Dutch settlement that had already been taken over by the British in Schenectady.

The inhabitants were surprised to see French soldiers pulling toboggans and using snowshoes, something they'd soon learned from their Algonquin friends. Realizing that these pathetic men posed no threat, the Dutch gave them meager supplies of food and blankets to help them get them back to Quebec. But soon, a skirmish broke out with the Mohawks and only one hundred of the five hundred survived, Andre among them. These exhausted troops, near starvation, went back to Quebec.

Andre had been fortunate enough to meet a Jesuit priest, Father Simon LeMoyne, on the journey back to Quebec. The priest was living among the five nations of the Iroquois confederacy around Onondaga Lake.

In 1615, Samuel Champlain and his friends, the Hurons and Algonquins, had attacked the Iroquois stronghold, but had failed to conquer them. They remained enemies for forty years.

Over time, a number of Iroquois were converted to Christianity and sent a delegation to Montreal to request that a priest be sent to them. Father LeMoyne, taking his life in his hands, went to preach to the Onandagas, recognizing that this could be a move toward peace with the Iroquois. Through his exceptional diplomatic skills and sincerity, he gained their confidence. He planned to stay for a few days and ended up staying for several months. When he met Andre and the exhausted band of men, he was happy to share food and to help guide them back to Quebec.

While the men chewed the meat voraciously from large venison bones and sucked their fingers, Father LeMoyne spoke as he sat among them dressing their wounds.

"When I heard that *Huronia* was destroyed, I resolved to return. All I could remember was that beautiful village surrounded by fields of maize surrounded by plum trees and woods full of hares and partridge. I pictured its longhouses made of bark, numbering more than fifty. Each house was inhabited by three or more families. I remember the women and children running out to greet me. I resolved to see the destruction for myself.

On my trek back to *Huronia*, I stopped to drink from a spring near Lake Onondaga. My native guide shouted at me to stop drinking it for it was bad water and a spell had been cast on it by an evil spirit. I realized that it was salty and stayed behind to harvest some salt from it to carry back to Montreal." With that, Father LeMoyne pulled a small leather sack from his pocket and poured some of the rough crystals into Andre's hand. "I chose that site as a French settlement and I hope to return with some of our countrymen to harvest the salt. It's not unlike harvesting maple syrup. It takes huge quantities of wood for the fire, and lots of water before you get the water boiled down and enough crystals to dry."

With the help of the good father and the additional stores of food, the men reached Quebec without further difficulties, but their troubles were not over, for when they arrived, they found that a type of Spanish flu had spread from farm to farm, reducing the population.

At the end of summer, there were crops to be harvested and too few workers remained. The soldiers were recruited to work for farmers who would be responsible for their salaries.

Andre and three other members of the regiment were seated at a rough table at one of the farms eating venison stew after having cut wheat under the hot sun for an entire day.

"At least we won't starve here. I no longer feel my ribs when I rub my hands along my chest." He addressed the farmer's youngest daughter as he raised his bowl. The next day, he didn't have to ask. She gave him generous helpings and brought bread for the four.

His three companions shared a room in the farmhouse, but he declined the farmer's hospitality, for he'd become accustomed to the night air.

One night, as Andre lay asleep in the lean-to meant for animals in winter, he was awakened by a rustling sound. Alert after his experience with the Indians, he sat up, but it was only the farmer's youngest daughter whose name he didn't know who slid down beside him and covered them with a light blanket that she'd brought from the house.

"I thought you'd find it a bit cool out here alone," were the only words she spoke. His remaining nights would not be cool again.

After the harvest, the farmer paid them. This alleviated the problem of money for both the soldiers and the government, but paying them on time was always a problem.

Later, the regiment built strongholds along the Richelieu River, the Iroquois traditional route. Fortunes had been made with the great alliance between the French and Indians. The Iroquois, always allied with the British, were cut out of it. Controlling river transportation was the key.

A governor, a bishop and an *intendant* ruled Nouvelle-France, all appointed by the King. The *intendant* shared power with the governor and was in charge of the colony's finances. When the troops arrived, Monsieur De Meubles held that post. He was a creative and skillful manager. When faced with a continual lack of funds, he finally resorted to gathering up as many decks of playing cards as he could find. By putting a number on the back of a card he determined its value, thus creating a system of paper money. The cards were used in commerce and to pay salaries with the understanding and faith that they could be exchanged in the future for gold or silver. Unfortunately, even at the end of Monsieur De Meubles appointment and well after his return to France, the system continued, for it was always easy to issue more playing cards, and inflation resulted. The young colony was in a perpetual economic struggle, for there was always too much paper money and too few goods.

Meanwhile in Paris, Catherine thought that after more than two years Andre must surely have married. She'd had no word from him nor had she expected to. How could she know that he was an exhausted soldier trying to keep warm, fed, and clothed, not knowing what his next assignment would be?

That last time, so many months ago, after saying his goodbyes to

Andre, Papa had returned to his workshop and left them alone for a moment.

Though they'd never spoken about a future together, before leaving, Andre had asked for a memento and she gave him her handkerchief trimmed in lace with her initials embroidered on it. Slipping it in his doublet he'd brushed his lips lightly upon her hand and said goodbye.

Her thoughts returned to the day in the park when she'd first seen the notice. She had overheard a young woman, an orphan girl that she'd seen begging on the street, telling the girl beside her that she would go immediately to sign up.

"Nothing can be worse than my life has been these six months on the streets of Paris, begging for food, sleeping in alleyways, escaping men who pursue me for sexual favors. Trying to keep clean and warm is almost impossible, and I pray to God and the Virgin to keep me pure." Some of the other girls said they'd go just for the adventure, but they all seemed to have one thing in common: they were all poor.

CHAPTER 5
THE SHIP SAILS

Catherine wept as she walked up the gangplank in line with thirty-five other young women, all carrying bundles of about the same size. As they reached the deck, they stopped before a large table where each was given a case containing a bonnet, a silk handkerchief, gloves, stockings, shoelaces, thread, ribbons, needles, pins, scissors, two knives and two pounds in cash by the King's agent stationed there.

Some of them were not more than children. Then she realized that the youngest were the orphans of the Church of Notre Dame from rue *des* Archives, *Les enfants bleu*. These nameless girls were part of the colorful scene in Le *Marais*, a busy Parisian neighborhood. The boys were called *Les enfants rouge*. Both were recognizable by their blue or red shirts.

Catherine wouldn't turn her head to look back at her mother and sisters until she reached the top deck, in hopes that by then the tears would have stopped and she'd be able to wave her handkerchief and at least pretend to smile.

She remembered her mother's words the night before she left, when they had prayed together. Catherine had prayed that the Lord would give her courage to marry a man that she'd yet to meet. Her mother replied, "Remember, Catherine, love comes after marriage.

Do your best in all things and remember your dear Papa and me."

She had stroked her daughter's long, dark hair and looked into her eyes, those eyes of deep blue that her husband had passed on to all three of their daughters and almost in a whisper, she said once more, " Love comes after marriage."

The string on her bundle cut sharply into Catherine's hand as she tried to manage the new case. In the other, she carried a basket with freshly baked bread, a few apples, and some salted meats. She had a jar of water and cheeses wrapped in cloth, several linked sausages and a pot of pate. She knew the sacrifices made by her family to provide her such luxuries.

On the dock, her family clung to each other and looked so small huddled around their uncle who had also come to see her off. *Maman* had lost weight since Papa's death and Catherine didn't like the sound of her constant cough. Catching sight of her on the deck, they shouted her name and waved furiously. Catherine in turn waved and called out her goodbyes. She pulled her rough cloak closed and hurried to find a place below.

Her courage these past weeks had come from her resolve to help her family. It would be tested in the new land where a prospective husband was waiting.

I'll write to them often, and I'll try to earn extra money with my mending and knitting. I must succeed. These were her thoughts now as she arrived on board, but soon other things drew her attention.

The girls were milling about. She climbed down the narrow ladder that led below, careful to avoid tripping on her long cloak.

Much to her surprise, there were other occupants: chickens, pigs and rabbits that seemed as disoriented as the girls. There would be fresh meat on board, at least for a while. The smells were terrible and they hadn't even left port yet.

So, this was the *Golden Eagle*. It creaked and groaned and bore no resemblance to the name scrawled on its side, its letters difficult to make out. Would she suffer from miasma? What diseases lurked in this noxious air? She would have to stay healthy. She was glad of the extra pounds that *Maman* had encouraged her to gain for the journey. It would take three months before they reached land. Reports from other ships that had gone before included the bad news that as many as ten out of a hundred women died before reaching shore. Some ships had been attacked by pirates.

She prayed for good weather that would enable them to spend part of their days on the upper deck.

Below deck she had hoped for a cubicle at the very least, but what she saw was a vast raw space in the center of the hold. There were a few berths made of rough planks not more than five feet long for sleeping; and to keep the passengers from being tossed about. She decided she preferred a pallet on the floor.

Catherine smiled when she recognized the orphan girl that she'd met that first day when they'd stood before the notice. That time seemed so long ago now, though it had just been a few months. And behind her was the young widow who'd been in line ahead of her when she'd gone to the agent to register. She walked toward them and beckoned them to join her in hopes that the three could find a corner in the hold to spread their blankets before everyone else got there.

She wanted to avoid proximity to the animals with panic in their eyes. Suddenly, she had to pee. Buckets were set up behind a large block of wood. She put down her basket and asked the girls to wait. She held her breath. At least she was one of the first. It would be the most comfortable time that she'd have to relieve herself for the duration of the voyage.

The old ship squeaked and groaned and chains rattled as they left the dock, setting off a most alarming counter-squeal from the pigs. The girls stood shifting from foot to foot to maintain their balance as the ship set sail, turned and headed north.

Reluctantly, the women left their parcels and baskets, covering them with quilts and ran up to the deck to watch Paris and all that they knew recede in the distance as the *Golden Eagle* headed up the Seine to Normandy and their voyage across the sea.

CHAPTER 6
THE JOURNEY

T
he crew of the ship was warned that these women were to be protected. It was important that they reach Quebec safely, for not until they set foot on land would the shipping company receive compensation. Extra stores were on board, but luck was what they would need, for the weather was unpredictable and could add weeks to the journey.

Catherine had chosen her friends well. Charlotte, the orphan girl, buoyed by her decision to leave France and her miserable life, exhibited a delightful character. She seemed excited about the journey in contrast to the rest of the women. Orphaned at sixteen she'd lost not only her parents, but also her whole family.

Her parents had died of smallpox. She and her two brothers and one sister were vaccinated with the pus taken from the wracked body of her dear mother. She alone had survived the disease. She had lived with relatives for short periods of time but no one would take her in permanently. She had swept sidewalks in front of shops for a few coins, and had lived in doorways and begged for enough food or money to sustain her. This much she had chosen to tell her new friends.

Men had done terrible things to her in her last days in Paris when she had no money for food. Those terrible things she would try to forget and she would pray to God for forgiveness for she had gone willingly with them driven by hunger.

Her other friend, Marie Therese, was a widow. She wasn't much older than Charlotte. Her young husband had died of lockjaw. They were both twenty at the time, and had no children. She had worked for a fishmonger until now and hoped for a better future.

The three women talked and crocheted, and enjoyed each other's company. They took great pains to keep their space orderly and told stories to pass the hours. Their conversations often turned to the potential men who were waiting for them.

"What kind of man do you want, Catherine?" Without waiting for an answer, Charlotte continued, "I want a man who is strong and rich enough so that we'll never go hungry or lack for anything. I want my children to have a better life than I have had." Charlotte liked to play a game where they made up ideal men for themselves and for others. "Some of the men are rich already. There are fur traders who have built houses that are quite grand." The other women rather doubted that, but they left Charlotte to her dreams. However, Charlotte would be proven right, for great fortunes had been made by some.

Marie Therese mentioned women kidnapped by Iroquois men. "I wonder what it was like, especially for the children who were raised by the savages?"

Catherine who had always listened to Papa's stories and his news of Nouvelle-France was happy to tell them more about Monsieur Champlain. "He had many friends among the Hurons. He even sent Nicolas Vigneau, his youngest and favorite man whom he called 'my boy' to live with them and learn their language.

Mr. Champlain returned to France with two young Huron men, for the King was very interested in these people with whom he hoped to form an alliance against the Iroquois who controlled the fur trade. At Versailles, the Indians were as fascinated by the costumes of the

French as the French were with them, for all were dressed in their finery, the French with lace, silk, wigs and cosmetics and heavily perfumed, the Indians in soft leather, beads, feathers from rare birds and painted skin.

When Champlain returned to Quebec, two hundred Hurons were there to greet him with Nicolas, who was dressed like them.

Later, Mr. Champlain was shocked to find that much of the information that Nicolas had given him was false. He had reported that he'd gone as far as an ocean to the west, knowing that Champlain was searching for a route to Asia and would travel west with him. In reality Nicolas had stayed with the Hurons and had deceived Mr. Champlain because he wanted to return to live with the Indians.

"Maybe I would like to meet such a man and to hear his stories," Charlotte said.

"Perhaps you should read Mr. Champlain's diaries," Catherine suggested.

Charlotte wouldn't give up and added insistently, "But he didn't live with the Hurons. I want to know of the lives of the women and children. Did Nicolas write a diary?"

Catherine sat quietly remembering her father. The others became silent too. More than anything, they watched over each other.

The first weeks were bearable. The weather held and they exercised regularly by walking the small deck. Only a few girls at the time were allowed to do so. The sailors taught them to stare at the horizon and to move as though they were steering the ship to get over their seasickness. They caught rainwater and had enough to wash the salt air from their faces and to drink, but as the first month ended, storms became more frequent and instead of showers, they had downpours and heavy winds that kept them below for days. They hoped that their journey would not be extended for there would be the danger of running into icebergs. It was the beginning of the Little Ice Age.

The stench from the buckets and the animals made breathing difficult. Charlotte developed painful boils on her thigh that made it necessary for her to sit leaning to one side, and everyone on board had dysentery. Toward the end of the journey, they had sores in their mouths and bleeding gums from lack of fresh vegetables. Some of the girls were shocked when their teeth became so loose that they lost a few. Their legs swelled and they had no strength. Eating corned pork was so painful that they often ate only codfish and barley groats. Luckily, one sailor who had spent time in Nouvelle-France had learned to make a broth from the bark of an evergreen. It was a drink taught to him by a Mohawk friend. He shared some with the girls for he always carried a bundle of the bark onboard. At first, most of the women would not drink it, but seeing that those who did began to feel stronger, as the sores on their mouths healed, the rest agreed to partake.

After the first month, the animals were gone. The chickens appeared in stews as soon as they stopped laying. Then, there were none. Though there was relief from their noise and smells, that meant no more meat or eggs.

Marie Therese had a natural talent for healing and the herbs that she brought gave some relief to others, but several of the younger girls died after developing fevers. In spite of heavy rains, everyone went on deck to pray, and to say goodbye as their small bodies wrapped in canvas were given over to the sea. Saddest of all were the deaths of the fourteen-year-old orphan twins, Sarah and Sofie. They'd often come to Catherine and her friends to listen to stories and play games. The women looked after them to the best of their ability for they were the youngest on board. But they developed dysentery, and they became thinner day-by-day until the end. Marie Therese prepared their small bodies. Many prayers were said over them before they called to the sailors to carry them to the deck. Catherine, remembering her own young sisters whom she'd left behind, wept long into the night.

CHAPTER 7
NEW FRANCE-
THE ARRIVAL

Marie Therese rushed down the ladder from the deck. She shouted to the girls, "There are small birds on the rails. That has to mean land or at least an island!" Several of them rushed up on deck to ask the sailors. She was right, for two days later, the call of "Land ho" rang out from the crow's nest.

In spite of the hardships they'd endured and the friends they'd lost, the women became excited as their small ship sailed around the Gaspe Peninsula and into the Gulf of St. Lawrence. They would reach Quebec in another day.

In early morning of the next day, the ship entered the port of Quebec on the great St. Lawrence River, which is more than twenty miles wide at its mouth. Had they not been busy with preparations for landing, the women would have seen the magnificent Montmorency Falls dropping hundreds of feet into the river as the ship sailed past to its destination.

Though the women were weak, in the hours prior to the landing they made every effort to look their best. They scrubbed with fresh water from the river to remove the lice that were a constant problem and helped each other to comb them from their hair. Thankful for the bright sunshine, they had spread their best dresses on the deck or on lines for a few days to freshen them from the mould and mildew that covered everything.

A few hours later, from the deck they saw a number of small, rough buildings made of bark in the distance. Small fishing boats dotted the harbor along with forty-foot canoes. There were several large wooden houses as well, against a backdrop of mountains that loomed overhead.

The captain, taking Catherine's arm, pointed out the house of the governor, which looked like a fortress. "Look at that, will you? From that house, he probably has one of the best views in the world. I've never seen anything like it in my travels."

They would soon set foot on land. The women shared lip rouge and painted their cheeks, for they wanted to make a good impression on whoever would be waiting on shore. Rumors had arrived before them that a number of the girls had been prostitutes in France. Those in charge of the venture vehemently denied such stories. An earlier ship carried three classes of women. The *demoiselles* were meant for the Carignan-Salieres soldiers from the four companies kept in garrison, some of whom became colonists and received a land grant and a hundred pounds. Other women were meant for the few large landowners and the last group for the farmers.

As a crowd gathered on shore in anticipation of their arrival, one of the Ursuline Sisters, from the convent founded by Mrs. De La Peltrie, a rich young widow from the village of Alencon in France, overhearing such gossip was quick to retort. "Most of these young women are poor and perhaps hungry. We'll bring them back to health and they will be fertile. That's what our country needs."

There was pressure on the unmarried men who would be fined if they didn't select a bride within three months, and a reward of twenty pounds if they would marry before the age of twenty. The women were assured that they also would have a right to choose a proper spouse.

The women had all lost weight on the journey and their dresses, though their best, hung from their bodies. The dresses had full skirts, and most were silk or solid-colored wool with puffed sleeves and collars and cuffs of lace or velvet. They all wore the new simple head coverings of white cotton or lace, or white bonnets that they'd received upon boarding ship. They combed their hair and wound strands around their fingers to make ringlets that would frame their faces. They wore gloves made of pigskin or cotton.

One of the orphan girls, Madeleine, was feverish and her face, neck and arms were gently bathed with rainwater. Then, she was dressed by her companions. A sailor offered to carry her to shore.

Catherine and the other women walked down the ramp, unsteady after the long voyage. Some knelt and thanked God for their safe arrival. They looked around them in awe. Never had they seen such a primitive environment. They gazed at the small stone buildings and even smaller buildings made of wood enclosed in a stockade. The streets were muddy paths.

There were vast forests in every direction. Closer, were the large wigwams covered in bark that they'd glimpsed from the ship. Now, families could be seen going about their daily life. Smoke came from openings in the roofs of these large houses that could accommodate several families. These were the homes of the Hurons who were converts to Catholicism. When their own medicines proved ineffective against the new diseases, and the Iroquois had decimated their villages, weakened and sorrowful, the Huron men, women and children who remained, followed the Jesuits. These clergymen preached of an all-powerful God. Perhaps He could save them.

At first, the sick overwhelmed the hospital *Hotel Dieu*, run by the Sisters, but when it seemed that everyone who entered died, they ceased to trust the medicine of the Jesuits' God.

On the wharf, the newly arrived women continued to gaze about them, stunned by what they saw. The settlement looked so small and unprotected. Could they survive this change? A few knew immediately that it wouldn't be possible, and began pleading to return to France, in spite of the horrendous journey they'd just made. But most, realizing the limit of their choices, accepted this ground as their future home.

Some of the men whom they had seen from the ship were *coureurs du bois*. These were fur trappers, some of whom, from noble families, had come to seek adventure and shared a life of trapping and hunting with the Indians. There were farmers, the *habitants*, bearded and dressed in ragged clothes, sometimes made of leather or soft deerskin. They carried firearms.

A few uniformed soldiers and a number of men who were dressed quite formally, had also come to greet the ship. Also among them were the Jesuits dressed in faded black for there was a seminary in Quebec for Huron boys. Many of the men came forward to help the women with their bundles.

Seeing the men in uniform, Catherine's thoughts turned to Andre. Could he possibly be among them? Would it be he who would receive her dowry? Perhaps he was already married. Had he married a woman who came on an earlier ship? But there were so few… She tried to put these thoughts out of her mind, yet her eyes continued to scan the crowd. Andre with his kind manner and good looks would easily have found someone. Perhaps he'd married an Algonquin woman. Catherine had read memoirs written by some of the nuns. They had taught many of the girls to read and write and to keep house in the French manner. Some of the girls were given to the Jesuits to serve them. Could that have happened with Andre as well? It was a vast country and if he'd survived the skirmishes, he was in it somewhere, but not here and not now.

The day was beautiful and the air crisp and sweet. Several of the Ursuline Sisters were there to meet them, lending an air of civility to the moment. They had been the first novices to arrive when the convent opened in 1639. The exhausted women were taken there, directly followed by the men who carried their baggage. There, Mrs. De La Peltrie, the founder of the convent, appeared to greet the new arrivals, and the men departed.

Baths were prepared along with clean clothes and hot meals. To Catherine and the other women from the ship, never had a bath felt so luxurious, and never had a simple stew with large pieces of venison and vegetables tasted so delicious. Waiting for it to be ladled into her bowl, the delicious aroma reached her first and it was indeed mouth watering. She forced herself to eat with some restraint and smiled when she was offered more.

The Sisters, skilled nurses, attended the sick. But Madeleine, whom the sailor had carried ashore, died by morning. The poor young woman was buried in her best outfit and her only pair of shoes and stockings. Her bundle contained her remaining clothes, a shabby, patched dress, a nightdress, her new pair of gloves and a muff made of dog skin. At least she'd been spared burial at sea and was put to rest in the small cemetery behind the church.

Marriages were arranged within days by the efficient Sisters who had done this before, for several ships had arrived in the previous year. A few of the young girls were allowed to stay at the convent until they reached the age of sixteen. The dedicated nuns had come to this land to save souls, primarily those of the savages, but these new arrivals would soon provide more souls to whom they would teach the word of the Lord.

As soon as a contract was signed in front of a notary, the girls received part of their dowry, a chest, a pot, some tools, pins, two changes of clothes, headscarves, combs, handkerchiefs, ribbons, and a cask of port. Sometimes even livestock was included, but first, they were given one hundred francs to pay their passage from Europe, all gifts from the King's treasury. Louie XIV was determined that this venture in *Nouvelle-France* would succeed and gold poured from the treasury to the landlords, government officials, militia and the clergy.

Usually, a civil marriage ceremony came first, to be followed by a religious ceremony when it was convenient. All of the women were Catholic. Protestants were not accepted, for the royal families of France and England were still enemies, warring over religious issues as well as battling over land ownership. This would continue in the new land.

Catherine's first introduction was to Etienne. He was a sturdy young man, a farmer. In Normandy he'd worked as a surveyor, a skill that was needed here. He'd been given a large tract of land. He had a good face and at their first meeting, he had requested her as his bride.

Along with the other girls, she remained at the convent for several days during which time the women were introduced to some of the skills that they would need in this new land as they helped the Sisters with soap-making, candle-making, and weaving. They were introduced to new foods as well. Bear stew with corn was one of the dishes, and they learned that pease porridge was an important staple in times of food shortages. Their prospective husbands were welcome to visit.

About a week after their arrival, on a day when the women and men were gathered in the large social room at the convent, Mrs. De La Peltrie visited once again.

Now, approaching fifty, she was a central figure in Quebec life. She lived in a small house on the grounds of the convent with her servant. She greeted everyone with enthusiasm.

"I've been here for over twenty years. It's a hard but rewarding country. Please visit my school for Indian girls, but don't be surprised by my students. I provided them with clothes and taught them to dress like us, but their wild ways took over." The women in the room listened with interest. She continued, " I accept them as they are in their deerskin clothes and their beads. They are lovely girls and quick learners. I've learned from them as well, for now I speak their language." Her achievements were known in France as well as *Nouvelle-France* for she was her own best advocate and wrote articles about her achievements that were widely read.

Did she and the good Sisters and Jesuits know that Indians were not eager to part with their beloved children? To satisfy the requests of the Jesuits for young girls to convert and educate, they sometimes kidnapped girls of other tribes. Slavery had been practiced among tribes for many years and the Indians would give some of their slaves to the French as gifts or in trade.

The Sisters and the men were surprised to find that most of the girls from *The Golden Eagle* on this voyage, were city dwellers, and quite pretty A few could read and write and the rest could at least sign their names. On later voyages, Mrs. De La Peltrie determined to send a representative to France to make the selections. Strength and experience in a rural environment would prove more valuable. In future years it would be said that the Quebec women were the prettier, for they were the first to come and had city ways.

These women were surprised in return by the amount of hard labor that would be expected of them. Many a young bride found herself pulling the plow while her husband steered with one hand and held a gun in the other. Beasts of burden were rare in this land and expensive. The land grants were far apart and the isolation afforded little protection. The women and children would also be trained in the use of a gun.

Catherine did not request another introduction. Trusting her judgment, she accepted Etienne, for though he was shy, she felt his humility, and his strong hands reminded her of dear Papa's.

And what were his thoughts as he looked at this woman who was almost his height and whose rich brown curls framed her face? He dared not look into her blue eyes and instead focused on a space above her left shoulder.

His voice quavered as he spoke. "I have built a two-room cabin with an outhouse. The corn and some vegetables are already planted. The soil here is very rich, but the growing season is short. This year, the maple syrup ran well and I have several gallons of syrup, tins of maple butter and loaves of sugar, enough to last until next spring. I have just built an outdoor oven. Perhaps you will be happy for it when you bake bread."

"Thank you. I will try my best to be a proper wife." She could think of no other words for the moment.

Not all of the women were so complacent. Several women agreed to a mate and then changed their minds, sometimes promising themselves to two or three men before making a final decision, while others would demand an annulment after several months of marriage.

A few days later, at their civil ceremony, Catherine was given fifty-five francs. What had happened to the two hundred francs advertised in the notice? The woman beside her received twenty-five.

"How were these dowries decided?" she wondered, but no answer was forthcoming. Etienne received the dowry, and together they walked to their home. For more than an hour, she followed him down the muddy path that led to his cabin. He carried the chest strapped to his back, and she, her bundle of clothes. He would go back for the cask of port another day.

She wore a cotton dress provided by the sisters that was considerably shorter than she would have worn in Paris, but was glad for it when she saw the mud, for it had rained heavily the previous night. They both wore leather moccasins. The wooden shoes worn by so many in France were not suitable on this land and Catherine had packed away the delicate leather slippers that her father had made for her.

Approaching the dwelling, she was startled as a large sow came around the corner. "Don't worry. She won't hurt you. She is very friendly, just like a dog. I'll put her back in her pen. She has learned to loosen the boards and comes out to visit occasionally."

The door to the cabin was open. There was a dish on the table that contained large blackberries. There was also a water pitcher. "I'll get fresh water. We have a wonderful spring very near the house."

She gazed around her. There were two ladder back chairs with rush seats. A shelf on one wall held a few mugs and dishes. The house was plain and clean. A homemade broom rested in the corner. The village seemed so far away.

At the convent, she'd heard that Indians, friendly at first when dealing with trappers and hunters, had become disturbed by the amount of encroachment on their lands as more settlers arrived and built homesteads. Peace treaties were signed with Algonquins and Hurons, but the Iroquois Nation that consisted of many tribes including the Senecas, the Mohawks, the Oneidas and others, were allies of the British. There had been attacks on settlers in the past year. Women never knew if their husbands would return from the fields and whole families were sometimes attacked.

She'd also heard of the work of the Carignan-Salieres Regiment and the forts they were building along the New York border, the Iroquois water route.

Catherine sat quietly surveying her new home. She looked out through the open door and watched several chickens that roamed around freely, pecking the ground and stopping every few minutes as if frozen, giving sideways glances in anticipation of what? She didn't know. Then, they'd return to their pecking. Their clucking was the only sound she heard.

Etienne returned carrying water and a small bucket of fresh milk from the cow that he'd raised from a calf. He'd received her in trade for building a fence for a friend. "You're enjoying the chickens, eh? I'd better get them in the fenced in area or we won't have them to enjoy. The raccoons like them too, and so do the foxes and the hawks."

When he came back in from this chore, Etienne took out two tin plates and two roughly made spoons. Pouring milk over the berries and stale bread, he noticed Catherine looking down at the dirt floor.

"Soon, I'll lay a proper floor. I'm waiting for boards from another *habitant* who cut some of my trees. It should be done before winter."

Then, he picked up a large lump of maple sugar and broke some over each serving, adding the few remaining berries.

Heads lowered, they said a silent, simple blessing that joined them spiritually for a moment. They made the sign of the cross. Neither of them spoke during the meal.

Leaving the dishes on the table, he motioned her to the other room. It contained a rope bed made of hand-hewn logs, and a corn-husk mattress. There was a row of wooden pegs on the wall where his few clothes hung.

On the bed was a coverlet of blue and white. "My mother wove this blanket herself. It's one of the few household things that I brought from Dieppe, and that picture of the Sacred Heart of Jesus." He looked at her pleasantly,

"It's the first time I use the coverlet."

He pulled the blanket aside and motioned her to sit down. She sat on the edge of the bed. He removed her shoes and stockings and stood expectantly, pointing to her dress. Blushing, she raised herself and pulled it over her head. She put her legs under the covers and turned her back to him. She heard his trousers drop to the floor. His breathing became heavy as he removed his shirt. He climbed in beside her and pressed against her.

She remembered hearing her parents and the muffled sounds that came from their bed before her father's illness. She hadn't known if they were expressions of pleasure or pain. She looked up at the picture on the wall and stared into the eyes of the Sacred Heart of Jesus. Then, she slowly turned to face Etienne.

CHAPTER 8
THE WINTER

In the small looking glass that she'd placed in the bedroom, Catherine hardly recognized the young Parisian girl she'd been. She had gained weight. Her tan color was not unflattering, though it would have been shocking in Paris. She glanced out the window and saw Etienne chopping wood.

"So this is the man that I will spend the rest of my life with," and a smile appeared on her face. Few words passed between them as they planted, harvested, and tended the animals.

Etienne often couldn't resist an affectionate slap on her *derriere* as she passed by.

She noted nature's surprises, both good and bad. Catherine was pleased by the abundance of wildflowers, berries and songbirds. Yet, there were periods after a rain in which mosquitoes buzzed mercilessly above the heads of every living thing. The black flies that bit the flesh without warning drove her into the house where even there she found little respite, for they had no windows.

In autumn, the trees turned the most glorious reds and golds—colors that appeared to melt into the lakes. As she took their small boat down river to fish to provide food for fast days when meat was forbidden, she imagined herself a painter as she dipped her oars into the myriad colors. Looking up, the tall maples seemed aflame as they reached the blue sky above.

Suddenly, she heard a loud bellow. It was almost earthshaking. She had no idea what animal could make such a sound. She reached for the gun that Etienne insisted that she carry any time she went away from the cabin, but then, on shore, she saw a huge animal. Too big to be a cow, she realized it was a female moose. Beside her was a smaller animal, her calf. She bellowed again and again. Catherine stood watching.

Minutes later, out of the brush came another moose with enormous antlers. As soon as he was in sight, the female started walking away slowly. He followed hesitantly. Each time she stopped to graze, he came closer. Finally, he was close enough to rest his head on her haunches. The female paused for a moment, then continued to walk away. He caught up with her once more, this time laying his head across her neck and then rubbing against her face. The calf followed some distance behind.

Catherine hypnotized by the scene, watched in utter silence. After some time, the male made an attempt at mounting, but again the female moved ahead. Determined, he tried once more and this time he succeeded. Catherine turned away in embarrassment and pulled the boat into the water. After a few minutes, the animals, unaware of her presence, walked away into the thicket. She would not tell Etienne.

She fished for a while, but shaken by her encounter with nature, she pierced the flesh of her catch on a pointed stick, tied the small boat to a nearby tree and started for home. It was later than she thought. She could almost tell time by the honking of geese as they flew past by the hundreds at dusk, on their way home to roost. Autumn brought even more of the buzzing flies and darkening days.

In November, the snow reached halfway up their only window. With the house thus blanketed and the piles of logs they had cut together in summer and autumn to feed their fire, the cabin was warm. They had built a makeshift sled to carry the logs closer to the house.

All of the lakes and rivers were frozen.

Catherine was surprised when Etienne announced that most of the animals would be slaughtered at the end of November. She stayed inside when the sow was killed and held her hands over her ears as she heard the animal's piercing screams.

He butchered the sow and not a bit was wasted. Later, Etienne came in with a bucket of warm blood and taught her how to make *boudin*, blood sausage, using the intestines and the blood. As she fried this meat, she thanked the animal for her sacrifice.

In summer, they'd risen with the sun to feed the animals and tend crops, but in the short winter days they spent more time inside. Here, she pieced together the early life of this quiet man. He had come to *Nouvelle-France* like her, under contract. He had received acreage on condition that he would stay and work the land for three years. At the end of that time, he had decided to stay on in the small homestead that he'd established. He felt he had the skills and the strength needed to make a life in this new land. He had gained a feeling of independence in spite of the tithes that he had to pay to the church.

"At first I worked for the *seigneur*. Do you know that those landowners wanted us to carry on the custom of *homage* here in Nouvelle-France? At first we accepted the custom as people had accepted it in France but, after a year of hard work, there was no way we were going to go to the lord's house and bow with our heads down on the ground to honor him as our master. I was glad when my three years were up and the land was mine. Only a third of the men stayed. The others took the first boat back to France. They were lucky to get away. Later, the King ruled that habitants could not return to France and that they'd lost their citizenship. The choice was mine, but it wasn't the case for many others."

His work as a surveyor would continue as more settlers came, enabling him to buy his land and more necessities. He had carpentry skills learned from his father. He built a loom for Catherine and she soon remembered the lessons she'd learned from *Maman* and began weaving.

Her mornings were filled with inside chores. There was laundry, cooking, and cleaning. The hardest task was soap-making after the slaughter of the animals. They had to use the fat they had rendered by cleaning it thoroughly. The smell was overwhelming so it was done outdoors. The lard was boiled with an equal amount of water until it was all melted. Then lye had to be made.

"This smell is horrible," Catherine complained when she joined Etienne, who'd been working some distance from her. He had saved wood ashes in a wooden frame set on a stone and placed hay and sticks on top.

"At least it is only once a year," he reassured her as he poured water over the ashes to make lye. Later, equal mixtures of both lye and rendered fat were boiled for hours in another kettle, until after cooling, a brown jelly formed. This soft soap was used by the ladleful to do laundry. The laundry required that many buckets of water be brought in and heated. Hard soap would be made for bathing, but they rarely bathed, and Catherine had brought some scented soap from France that would last a year or more.

In winter, Catherine's outside chores were fewer. In the evening, she knitted stockings and mittens by the fire. A large pot that she filled with water, dried peas and ham hocks, hung over the fire, cooking slowly.

Etienne sharpened tools and did carving. He even carved wooden molds with patterns of acorns and leaves for the butter that they churned and for the loaves of maple sugar.

"We'll be planting flax in the spring so you'll be able to weave linen. Also, I think I'll have enough money to buy a few sheep. If I don't have the money, I'll do some carpentry work in exchange for some lambs."

Catherine nodded her head and silently thought that it would be more work for her, but it would not be her task alone. The growing of flax required several people and Etienne would enlist the aid of his neighbors and even children to plant and harvest the tender plants. After ripening, they would be dried in the sun, turned, then combed to remove seedpods for the next planting. When dry, they would be wet again to soften the stalks. The fibers would be separated, and then combed again. After dividing the flax among the neighbors, the women of each household would have the job of spinning it into thread. It would take an entire day to spin two skeins.

A lean-to protected the cow from the blinding snow and they brought their chickens inside, as well as a young piglet, who shared a corner of the kitchen with the fowl.

The ox that Etienne brought home in early November would share space beside the cow. The animals, warmed by each other's bodies, had small clouds of moisture above their heads formed by their breath. Their long thick winter coats protected them from the winds and were decorated with tiny balls of ice.

The days were so short that Catherine felt that two-thirds of her life was spent in darkness. I'm thankful for the bayberries that I harvested in summer, she thought, remembering the late afternoons when she went off by herself to gather them, the sun warming her. When she had a pail full, she melted them down, and later when the wax rose to the top she would pick it off and store the pieces. After a while she was ready to melt them again to dip the wicks. By stringing six of them on a stick, she could dip that many at a time.

They sometimes used a tallow lamp fueled by animal fat to provide light, but she preferred the scent of bayberry with its memories of summer.

Their evenings were silent, broken only by short conversations and the sounds of the wild creatures that shared their wilderness. Screech owls and the howling of wolves punctuated the night and startled Catherine as she said her nightly prayers kneeling beside their bed. It was there that she thought of her family so very far away. She bowed her head and through her tears she prayed, "Please, dear Jesus and Holy Mother. Please keep them healthy and safe."

To reach their spring, Catherine and Etienne tied burlap around their legs and used snowshoes. They sometimes had to crash the bucket through ice to get water. Often, they just melted snow. Game was plentiful and a deer carcass hung from a tree, frozen in the winter cold. It would remain fresh until spring. There was a danger of bear or wolves carrying it off or even a large bobcat, though they usually preferred smaller prey. The couple was always vigilant, watching for tracks.

Their diet of venison, rabbit, pork, potatoes, dried apples and walnuts led them to crave peas and beans that would come in the spring. They had also stored squash and corn that they'd learned to grow from their Indian neighbors. Cornmeal was valuable for cornbread and fritters when flour was in short supply.

Etienne went ice fishing at the end of each day. There were a hundred and forty fast days and the church encouraged the settlers to supplement their diet with fish.

Unaccustomed to the short days and long, dark nights after her years in Paris, Catherine would have gone mad had it not been for the music of the settlement and the church services where she could meet her friends from the voyage and make new friends among the older settlers.

From November eleventh, their fast began in preparation for the birth of Christ. They ate no meat or cheese, nor did they consume alcohol. A few days before Christmas, Etienne butchered the remaining young pig for their Christmas feast.

Midnight Mass, a custom that they'd brought from France, broke the monotony. Their small church, covered in ice and snow, glowed as they approached in their sled, for there were hundreds of candles within and the parishioners walking toward it carried lanterns.

"There's a peddler in front of the church selling something. Stop please and I'll run ahead to see what it is." Catherine jumped from the sled and ran ahead to the peddler who was selling engravings depicting the nativity and broadsheets of Christmas carols. She paid him and returned to Etienne smiling, for she was reminded of the same custom in Paris. "Tomorrow we'll sing the carols. I'll hang the engraving above the table."

They went into the church eager to see the *creche* and to greet their friends. There would be two more masses, one at dawn and the Christmas day mass. It was the end of their fast and the beginning of fun until January 6, the day of Epiphany.

Friends would gather at each other's houses for food, singing, dancing and storytelling. There, they would serve their precious wine instead of beer and cider. It would not be watered down on these special days, for wine equaled culture and culture equaled France.

The second week in January, when Etienne opened the door to go to the spring, the sun came streaming in.

"Catherine, come here. You won't believe your eyes." Catherine who'd been busy preparing breakfast turned and ran to the door shielding her eyes from the bright sun. Looking out over the forests, she saw a sight that was dazzling. It was the January thaw, and an ice storm had turned the forest into a land of enchantment as far as the eye could see.

When she stepped outside later, she saw icicles decorating their humble little cabin. "Etienne, it's like a castle for a king and queen."

Later, when she was scrubbing clothes using a washboard and the harsh soap that she had made, she looked down at her rough, red, cracked hands and laughed at herself for feeling like a queen even for an instant. Were I a queen, I'd have to hide these hands beneath my cloak. She carried the tub outside; poured off the water; squeezed and wrung the clothes as best she could. Then, she draped the clothes on various bushes and low hanging branches, thinking of the amusing shapes that they would take on when frozen as she gathered them and brought them in to finish drying by the fire.

The next day, there was a quick freeze and when they went out to check the traps, there was such a thick crust on the snow that they didn't need snowshoes. Walking along gingerly, they began to slip and slide. Catherine wound her woolen cape around her tightly and slid all the way down the small hill to the edge of the woods, calling to her husband to do the same. That night she wrote in her diary for the first time since arriving in New France.

"Yesterday and today were magical for me. I have never seen anything as beautiful as the ice storm that we had. Not even the great cathedrals of Paris when they are lighted for Easter were ever as grand as our forest turned to diamonds. Today, my husband and I slid down the hill and I felt like a small child once again. I haven't laughed so heartily since before the death of my dear Papa. These were two very fine days and I thank God Almighty for them."

CHAPTER 9
SPRING

In March, when the sap began to run they doubled the amount usually gathered by Etienne for now they were two. He had carved extra taps during their quiet evenings and they placed barrels on a sled to carry the sap to the sugar shack where a fire was kept burning under giant kettles. Catherine secretly thought that they might have enough syrup and sugar to sell to the sailors. That would be a way to earn a few francs for *Maman*, but when she saw how little syrup was left after it boiled down, she realized that she'd have to think of some other way.

Their woodpile had diminished. It took many cords to boil the sap down. She had become as adept as Etienne at chopping wood and for the next few days they would devote their energies to making their woodpile grow.

Stopping to wipe her sweaty brow she said, "Etienne. I am twice warmed by this wood: once in the chopping and once in the burning." Then she thought of the baths they would take in May or June and the many buckets of water that would be needed to fill the large tub in front of their house. The woodpile would have to grow to heat the water. Her chopping became more vigorous.

She laughed to herself as she remembered the saying, "May bath,

June wedding." Pity the bride who marries in April! She continued chopping.

As the spring sun became stronger, she put out her washtub at dawn and let the clothes soak, knowing that the water would be warm by mid-morning. That made her washing task a bit easier, and gave her more time for baking bread and food preparation.

In Paris, she had learned to bake bread from her uncle, and had found none to compare with hers here in Nouvelle-France. She asked Etienne for permission to sell bread to the ship's crew before they sailed to France, and by June, she was able to send a few francs to her family. But, for the settlers, ever dominated by Church and State, even bread making was subject to rules. 'In addition to white bread and light bread, dark bread shall be made when herein required." Other much more restrictive rules were imposed. *Habitants* were not allowed to rent rooms in the city of Quebec without permission in writing. Public meetings were restricted; chimneys cleaned on command. There were limits to the size of farms, sub-divisions, numbers of horses owned. These rules, posted on the church doors, were read to the public or read from the pulpit. Punishments were cruelly carried out for torture was sanctioned. Rules came from the Church and the State. Speaking poorly of royalty was punishable as was profanity. The punishment for taking the Lord's name in vain was having the upper lip cut with a hot iron. For repeated cases of blasphemy, the person's tongue would be cut out. Murderers would be tortured, then strangled. Their bodies would hang in full view of the city for days.

The cow had calved, the sow had given birth and Catherine was pregnant. She knew that their sounds, hers and Etienne's, were sounds of pleasure. She worried that her enjoyment was sinful and prayed for forgiveness. She would lie quietly on her side of the bed anticipating his move toward her. Though Etienne, like her, worked from dawn to dusk, he had energy left to please her. His touches were soft and his thrusts had become gentle, unlike those of their early months together.

Their first child, a daughter, was born in late autumn. Etienne helped with the delivery. They named her Marie Elizabeth. When she was a month old, a Jesuit missionary christened her. Catherine's two friends from the voyage were at the church. Marie Therese was the baby's godmother and her husband, Francois, the godfather.

Little Marie yawned and stretched her arms. She was dressed in a lovely christening dress with cutwork and embroidery that Catherine had sewn months before her birth.

The dear baby awakened with a look of annoyance when the priest placed salt on her tongue and sprinkled holy water on her head. Then she went back to sleep, much to the amusement of her loving parents and their friends.

The Jesuit missionaries said mass every Sunday and performed baptisms, though Etienne and Catherine would usually attend only in good weather, and like most people, just four or five times a year.

Sometimes, on Saturdays in *Hotel de Ville* there would be dances. The violin was popular and musicians were on hand to provide lively entertainment. The people brought with them the reels, the balls and the ballets from France much to the disapproval of the clergy.

A few people were excommunicated for dancing, especially if on a Saturday they had dared to dance past midnight. The priests' intention was to 'hunt them down like wolves'. Superstitious, some believed that there was more to fear from the wrath of God than from the priests, and that blood flowed from the maple trees instead of sap when tapped by those who had danced on Sunday.

One evening, after a church service where the priest ranted about how women dressed and the evils of pleasure, Catherine sat silently for a long time.

"What's wrong," asked Etienne. "It's not like you to stare into the fire that way without a word."

Catherine answered, "I was just thinking about Paris. The priests didn't have so much power there. It seems that they rule us with an iron fist here in *Nouvelle-France*. It makes me uncomfortable. They seem to want to deny any of the simplest pleasures like dance and music."

"Watch yourself, Catherine. Keep your opinions here in our home. It's not your place to criticize the good priests. Don't put yourself in danger."

Catherine continued to gaze into the fire, but her face took on a look of stone rather than one of thought. She was not accustomed to being reprimanded by her husband.

Etienne had not told her, but a week before, while a dance was in progress, a man had stepped out to relieve himself. While behind the building, he discovered two sailors and one of the governor's guards performing immoral acts outside of the *Hotel* de *Ville*.

They were accused of buggery and ordered to return to France as prisoners. At that time in Quebec the usual sentence was burning at the stake so perhaps they felt their sentences to be lenient.

Some months earlier, a drummer boy was found with another young man. Etienne, who had been at the hearing recalled the document that was posted on the wall of the courthouse which included a description of the crime:

The accused were found in a haystack. Both men had their trousers open and down around their knees; one man was lying upon another who was face down.

The drummer boy was found guilty and given the following sentence:

"For your penalty, you may have a choice: you may choose to be burnt at the stake or you will agree to become the executioner for the court."

The young boy became the executioner.

Etienne did not relate the details of this case to Catherine, but the news reached her through the usual gossip that came from the city. Later, on the eve of her hearing it, she reproached Etienne. "I hope you didn't condone that penalty. It was barbaric to turn that young man into an executioner in spite of his crime."

Etienne remained silent, smoking his pipe. His only thoughts were of how flattering it was when color rose to Catherine's cheeks when she was agitated, and of how strong these women of Quebec had become.

In spite of restrictions, the dances continued, and the citizens enjoyed drinking and eating. In the course of an evening, many kegs of beer, and platters of venison along with pork pies and raisin tarts soon disappeared.

Etienne, usually content to sit and watch as Catherine danced, sometimes joined easier reels with their repetitive steps. Catherine was pleased that she could meet Marie Therese and Francois, and Charlotte and her husband, Joseph.

Charlotte never complained about Joseph, but as Catherine watched, she worried that he was too fond of drink. He often fell asleep during the evening, and staggered when they were leaving to go home.

CHAPTER 10
LONELINESS

In February, as the winter days grew longer, Etienne had more work as a surveyor which took him away from home for several days or even weeks at a time. He took a crew with him and they carried supplies into the dense forests. Once these supplies were gone, they relied on their hunting. Often, they trudged through many feet of snow and encountered wild animals. Occasionally, they came upon squatters who threatened their lives, not expecting anyone to be marking this land where they'd built humble shacks. He was called upon more and more as new people came.

This was a difficult time for Catherine. She felt lonely and overwhelmed, for the chores were unending. Though she was thankful for her dear little one, she often had to neglect the baby to take care of the animals during Etienne's long absences. But those absences meant more money to purchase land or goods for their home.

She met a young Huron woman who was willing to help her with her chores in exchange for pins and an iron cooking pot. Later, Catherine would share other goods with her. Educated by the Sisters, she spoke French. She brought her two children when she came to help. The older child, a boy, was three and the younger a daughter, less than a year old, was on her cradleboard.

"My name is Kineks," she said softly, "it means Rosebud and these are my children Howi and Chimali. My son Howi's name means Turtledove and my little girl Chimali's means Bluebird.

The sisters called me Rosebud. You may do the same if you wish."

Howi clung to his mother's deerskin skirt and peeked from behind her leg.

Catherine was amazed by how contented the children seemed. Little Chimali seemed perfectly happy on her cradleboard and her bright, dark eyes followed them about the room.

When Etienne returned, he asked her how Kineks could be helpful when she came with two children.

Catherine answered, "You can call her Rosebud if you like for she became accustomed to that name in school. The children? They're no problem at all. She often just props Chimali against the wall on her cradleboard and the child watches us with interest. Little Howi follows Rosebud and helps with the chores. You should see him feeding the chickens. It makes me so happy to have their little family around and little Howi likes to make our baby smile."

Catherine didn't realize that one thing was offensive to Rosebud and that was her smell and that of Etienne. The Indian family bathed frequently. They heated stones and placed them in a small enclosure. Naked, they sweated and rubbed their skin briskly. Then, winter or summer, they plunged into the river or lake to rinse. Rosebud saw no sign of bathing here. What strange people these Frenchmen were.

Two years later, another son was born to Etienne and Catherine, and sixteen months later, another. With three children, Catherine didn't have time to miss Etienne as his surveying jobs increased.

Their infant spent many hours in the hand- hewn cradle that his Papa had made for him.

Marie Elizabeth who was only four, looked after her two-year-old brother, keeping him away from the fire or distracting him with sticks and stones or with the rag dolls that their mother had made for them.

As the years went by, Rosebud continued to work for Catherine and they became close friends. Now, as she expected a fourth child, she wondered why Rosebud wasn't pregnant. Perhaps she was infertile, but Catherine never asked.

It was not uncommon for Indian women to take herbal medicine or to rely on the ceremony of a medicine woman to prevent further births, though these remedies did not always work. But the Indian women accepted the children gladly for they wanted large families.

"Since the diseases have killed most of her tribe, perhaps Kineks prefers to nurture the two little ones that she has," Catherine told Etienne.

Kineks' husband hunted to feed their family and occasionally worked in logging camps and did some trapping, but he'd fallen victim to the brandy that the traders were all too willing to sell to Indians. At the time of their marriage, he had moved into her family lodge as was their custom, but soon after the start of winter, within days of each other, all members of the lodge had died except for the young couple.

Now, Rosebud's little house, built by her husband, was modeled after that of the poorest *habitants*. It had a small garden planted with pumpkins and squash on the side and seemed like a lonely place after the wigwams that Catherine had seen from the ship when she'd first arrived in New France. At that time, as many as a hundred people lived in small communities and women could be seen performing their daily chores together while their children played happily among them.

Kineks would not allow the priests to visit their home for she believed it was they who carried the evil that had taken away her family.

One of the activities that the two women most enjoyed was the wild rice harvest. Rosebud called the grain *manomin*, but Catherine called it Canada rice. Etienne had received some as a gift from his native friends when he was in the forests and soon realized its value for, once harvested and dried, it could be stored indefinitely. In late August and early September, the lakes and rivers where the waters ran slowly were so thick with this crop that the boughs, now four feet high hung low and the desired seeds came from the topmost shoot of the plant.

In their canoe with one paddling and the person in the rear harvesting, they could gather many pounds of seeds. Etienne carved the two poles of cedar that they would need. One was used to bend the stalk and the other to tap the ripened seeds into the canoe. To find the best places for harvesting one needed only to watch and listen for ducks and geese for they would be feeding in these rich rice beds.

Other families joined Rosebud and Catherine in their canoes while some watched over the children and awaited their day to paddle through the grassy lake. When the canoe was full, the women returned home. Drying and threshing would come next, but the cherished day was the harvest.

CHAPTER 11
MONTREAL
A NEW LIFE: 1668-1689

Etienne and Catherine, pregnant once more, moved to *Ville Marie*, which would later be called Montreal. During their thirteen years in Quebec, she had given birth to nine children, but there were seven at the table. It had saddened her to leave the two tiny graves and how she would miss her dear friend Rosebud. They were as close as sisters and their children had grown up together.

In addition to his work as a surveyor, Etienne was now a notary, for Catherine had taught him to read during their quiet winter evenings. In exchange, she learned to do simple calculations. It was usual that men knew how to do sums, and Etienne's mathematical ability was superior to most. He had a sharp mind and an eager spirit. He soon performed his tasks as a notary with ease, though he sometimes asked Catherine to enter names in logs in her more refined hand. He was well respected and Montreal was growing.

Their new house in the center of town was built of stone and had ten rooms.

Catherine taught her children to read from an early age and often spoke to them about her parents and the family that she'd left behind in Paris.

Twelve-year old Marie Elizabeth helped with the children and all of the house chores. She was particularly talented at sewing and took on all the mending.

When she looked at her eldest child, Catherine saw her own father's cheerful blue eyes and capable hands. Originally from the fourth caste, that of shoemaker, he had risen to that of artisan, for when a member of the court had seen the shoes that he'd made, he'd received many orders from the Duc de Guise, the wealthiest man after the King, who lived just one street away in the Marais district of Paris.

She remembered her father, sitting on a three-legged stool, carefully marking out the precious leather without wasting an inch and cutting into it with care, and his glee as he showed the family the finished product, ready to be delivered to the royal court. No longer did he have to make shoes out of old ones that would sell in the market as "18 - twice nine and twice new," the exclamation of the shoe vendor.

She saw this same perfection and joy in a job well done in her eldest. "Maman, this is for Babette. Do you think she'll like it?" said Mary Catherine holding up a lovely dimity frock that she'd made for her youngest sister without the use of a pattern .

Catherine smiled and nodded, "She will surely be pleased. Of course she'll like it."

Placing her hands on her belly, she worried as the birth of this child approached. She was thankful for her good friend, Marie Demers, who was a mid-wife. She would need her help for she remembered that her last two pregnancies in Quebec had been difficult and the babies stillborn.

Mrs. Demers had nine children under the age of fifteen, and still found time to work as a midwife. She'd met Catherine at mass and had noticed her swollen belly. She asked how the pregnancy was progressing.

"I lost my last two babies early in my confinement. I pray to God that I won't lose this one."

Patting Catherine's arm gently, Mrs. Demers tried to stem her fears.

"We have fine midwives here and I'm one of them. Don't hesitate to consult me at any time if you're worried." Mrs. Demers had two servants who helped her with her large family.

The government of France was determined to populate New France. Neither she nor Catherine had reached the desired family size to be eligible for an annual stipend. One had to have ten living children to receive the sum of three hundred pounds from the government.

Twelve living children would bring four hundred pounds.

A few months later, in the middle of the night, realizing that her pains were close together, Catherine turned to Etienne, and whispered close to his ear that it was time. She had consulted Marie several times since their first meeting, and saw her frequently at church. She was comforted to know she would attend the birth.

Etienne saddled his horse and hurried to the Demers house.

Accustomed to these calls in the wee hours, Marie Demers rose immediately and followed him to his house in a carriage driven by her young servant, Armand.

In less than an hour, a healthy boy was born. Swaddling the baby, she placed him in his mother's arms and let her rest. Marie Elizabeth stayed by her mother's side. Except for Charles, her eldest son, the younger children slept through the event.

Mrs. Demers reminded young Charles to be sure to contact the three neighbors who would sit with Catherine and the new baby.

This had been pre-arranged with the idea that they would sit with her during her labor, as was customary, but the baby had come quickly and in the middle of the night.

After the birth, downstairs in the warm kitchen, Etienne poured a cup of tea for the midwife. He handed her the cup and saucer saying, "Rest here a while. The sun will be up soon."

"Thank you. I'll be glad for it." She blew on the tea that she'd poured into the saucer. "The baby and your wife are strong. There is nothing to fear."

Relieved, he joined her holding his mug of tea, and sat heavily in the rocking chair in front of the blazing fire.

He'd heard that her husband, Mr. Demers, had arrived in Quebec in the first migration, and he was eager to hear more about it, for Andre Demers and his brothers were well known in this small community. They were excellent carpenters and entrepreneurs. "Were you a dDaughter of the King?" Etienne asked.

"No, I arrived some years earlier with my father who was a master stonemason. He came in the recruitment. My mother died in France when I was born in 1636. Papa remarried here." Mr. Demers and his brothers came from Dieppe with their father in 1643," she said, referring to her husband in the formal manner. I was a widow you see. My first husband was killed in a logging accident the fifth year of our marriage. My second marriage was two years later in La Garenne in 1654, more than twelve years ago. I remember that day very well because it was such a cold February. I didn't even realize it at the time, but my cheeks were frostbitten though it was just a few minute's walk to the notary. I never met *Grandmere* Barbe, my mother-in-law for she stayed behind in Dieppe with their youngest son and an older daughter. The daughter, Mary Margaret, was a Huguenot you know. She converted for her husband. That brought shame to the family. Later, my husband heard that she and her family had escaped Dieppe, and gone to Erlangen, in Germany. Those poor people walked for weeks to get there. They were promised houses, shops and many benefits, but when they got there they found only fields. Later, the government of Erlangen kept its promises, but those heathens suffered a lot. They did build a church, though. When the *Edict* of *Nantes* was revoked, you see, the lives of all Huguenots were in danger. *Grandpere* was the ship's carpenter on *L'Esperance* and he sometimes brought us news.

In the early years of our marriage, we saw a lot of him. He made frequent crossings, but he encouraged his sons to stay in *Ville Marie*. He saw a future for them here, and he was right. From the beginning there was no end to their work after they'd built their cabins. *Grandpere* was in Montreal when our second son was christened. Then he returned to France and I don't think he'll sail again." She took a long draught of her tea. "Have you selected a name for the infant?"

Etienne and Catherine had decided together. "Our son will be named Alexis after my wife's father who died in Paris."

The christening might not take place for a year; many infants died before their first birthday.

"Tell me more about the work that your husband and his brothers did when they first arrived here."

"They built the church and several houses. The houses were rough structures but the church is something to behold. It is quite grand, don't you think?

Then there were the forts nearby. I think the beautiful *Notre Dame* de *Bonsecours* Chapel and the *Notre Dame* Basilica that they finished in 1656 were their greatest achievements."

She paused to drink her tea. "Our oldest son is building a house in lower Quebec now and his father is helping him. The house is made of stone and has lovely decorative mantels and moldings made of wood. It will be a very fine house when it's finished. Building the chapel gave my husband a lot of inspiration."

As Mrs. Demers paused, Etienne was satisfied that she'd answered his questions. Now, he was eager to go to see his new son, but she continued. "You are newcomers here. You'll soon meet our dear Mademoiselle Bourgeoys. Without her, we would never have had the chapel. She sailed here from the Champagne Region in February. Imagine leaving in the middle of the winter with all those icebergs floating about. She arrived in 1653. She was just a young girl, but by 1658 she had converted a stable into a school. We owe our fine social network to her. She even trained me to be a mid-wife, and because of her, we must be licensed."

She sensed that he was bored, "But now, I must return. I'm glad the birth went well and they are both healthy. You have *Mademoiselle* Bourgeoys to thank for that."

Nodding in agreement, he gave her a basket of sausage, jars of honey, precious tea, and a loaf of maple sugar. "Thank you for bringing our child into this world." He heard the faint cries of his newborn son as he walked her to the door.

"Perhaps there will be a new occupant in the cradle next year."

"God willing," was his answer. He breathed a sigh of relief as he closed the door and thanked God that Catherine wasn't talkative.

As their families grew, Catherine and the other daughters of the King would have large families with as many as sixteen children. Little Marie Elizabeth would be the eldest of twelve, and later, she herself would have sixteen children.

Armand, the young servant who'd been asleep in the small two-seater carriage, threw off the heavy buffalo robe, jumped to the ground and helped Mrs. Demers into the cart. He had been with her for three years since she'd taken him from the orphanage. A year later, his sister Francine joined him. The Demers family was very kind to them. He was thankful for their warm room, clothes and hearty meals. After finishing up their daily chores and cleaning up from supper, he and his sister slept on the floor in the kitchen close to the fire that had been banked for the night.

Now, with the sun just rising, they passed several new houses. Marie Demers had read the results of the census: Forty percent of the population was under the age of fourteen;

Two hundred and fifty-seven women were unmarried, but not for long. Some would become nuns, brides of Christ, but for the others, as soon as they reached the age of sixteen there would be marriages and more children.

Montreal had 760 inhabitants and more than 100 of those were members of the clergy.

Trois Rivieres, 602.

Quebec, 2,857.

La Nouvelle-France was growing with a total of 4,219 people.

Marie Demers herself had childbearing years remaining and would add three more children to the population of Montreal and a healthy annual stipend to their family income.

Their carriage passed the little house of Mademoiselle Bourgeoys of whom she'd spoken to Etienne. "She's away now, but I think she should return from France any day now," she said to Armand.

This ambitious woman would return from France with a wooden statuette of *Notre-Dame-de-Bon-Secours* for the chapel, and would soon found the order of the Sisters of Notre Dame.

CHAPTER 12
THE REUNION-1673

There was a greater feeling of security now in French Canada, for more Carignan soldiers had arrived on the *St. Sebastian* in 1665. After three years they were dismissed and given fiefs. The country would need more women.

In 1673 another group of young women arrived on The *Golden Eagle*, this time with a big surprise for Catherine. Her sisters had come as Daughters of the King. After resting in Quebec for two weeks, they boarded a ship that was taking some of the King's Daughters to settle in Montreal and Trois Rivieres.

Her sisters would return to Quebec City by boat, but they wouldn't miss this opportunity to see Catherine and to meet her family. It was over two hundred miles between the cities and in spite of a shortage of roads, *Nouvelle-France* had an amazing navigation route. It was possible to sail from the Atlantic Ocean to the St. Laurence River all the way to Louisiana via a network of waterways.

Catherine had never been able to send enough money home for their dowries. She wondered if their mother had given them the same message she'd given her many years earlier: "Remember, love comes after marriage." She glanced around her at her husband and children who had come in for the evening meal. She would be proud to introduce them to her sisters.

They had a marvelous reunion. The three sisters wept tears of joy. Between kisses on wet cheeks, there were exclamations about how they'd changed and how well they looked. Catherine couldn't believe that Yvette, her baby sister was now a young lady, and that Marie, who now called herself Marie Rose, was so elegant. They spoke of dear *Maman*, whose health was poor and who was living with her sister. Times were changing in Paris. Conditions were getting worse every day. Inflation was horrific and there were small riots breaking out in the streets. The women often heard their uncle, the baker, complain about the price of flour, for he had to change the cost of a loaf of bread every few days. For two years, the growing season had been dreadful and the crops meager, but rather than blame the weather, the citizens blamed the royalty. "We ordinary people eat bread and soup if we are lucky, but there are many cafes and coffee houses in Paris. The princes and courtiers frequent them to eat sorbets, crystallized fruits, hippocras, a cordial of wines and spices, and exotic fruits in brandy. They drink fruit juices and the finest wines. They give no thought to the hungry." Yvette had tears as she spoke these words. Marie Rose added, "There is news from the palace that King Louis eats four plates of soup, a pheasant, a partridge, mutton with garlic, two slices of good ham and a plate of cakes. That is one meal for our Sun King, but enough to feed a family of eight for more than a week! If they aren't feasting, they are playing games. The stories that come from Versailles are incredible."

But this day in the home of Catherine and Etienne, wine, saved for special occasions flowed and it was not mixed with water. They dined on roasted meats in abundance and ate delicious tarts. There was no shortage of food here in Nouvelle-France, and no shortage of gaiety and laughter. Until this moment, Catherine hadn't known if she'd ever see her sisters again.

Etienne welcomed his sisters-in-law warmly. They were delighted to meet their nieces and nephews.

After ten days, they boarded a ship to return to Quebec. Marie Rose and Yvette would be wed within eight weeks. Seeing for themselves that Catherine had found a good man who worked hard and had provided her with a comfortable life they felt reassured that they might be as fortunate.

At the time, none of them realized that Andre would be present at the next family gathering. His career as a Carignan soldier had ended when he lost an eye in battle. The accident happened when he was loading his musket and the powder exploded. Andre was given eight arpents of land, each arpent was about three quarters of an acre. He was also given an ox, chickens, two hundred francs, and a fine horse.

In 1665, King Louie sent two stallions and twenty mares from his royal stables to the colony. These superb animals came from Normandy and Brittany. Eight mares were lost in the journey. The survivors were strong stocky animals that were black or chestnut and extraordinarily fertile, producing a foal every year. Andre, who had proved his valor many times in Europe and in *Nouvelle-France* was honored to receive such a fine animal from the King's own breeding stock. The Indians who witnessed the unloading of the horses, stared in amazement. Later, they would refer to them as 'the moose of France.'

After building his small settlement of a house and several outbuildings for animals and tenant farmers, Andre's life as an adventurer called to him once more. Taking only his horse, he left his property in the hands of a trusted tenant farmer and went out in search of iron ore after hearing that mines had been discovered. He got as far as Trois Rivieres where the bogs were rich in this precious metal. A small village grew up around the industry. In one year, they extracted eight hundred tons of ore. It was arduous work. Men dug in the bogs and loaded ox carts. A single forge was made. The King wanted more, for France was always at war. The settlers were in need of it as well.

Andre profited greatly in the beginning and turned his share over to others, but the endeavor wasn't very profitable and it would be years before more forges would be built. He sold his property and built a large house in upper Quebec, prepared to live the life of a gentleman. With two horses and some livestock, he would be free to dabble in commerce.

Compared to the time of Catherine's arrival, it was quite a different scene that greeted the sisters when they docked in Quebec. Now there were many more wooden houses in Lower Quebec, as well as warehouses and factories and the palace of the treasurer of the colony. In Upper Quebec were the fortress that had been repaired and fortified and the governor's residence that was now much grander. The religious and administrative buildings had new additions.

The two women, standing on the ship's deck were surprised when among the crowd they caught their first glimpse of their former neighbor, Andre Gervais. He was dressed in fine clothes and wearing a hat, and just eight weeks later, he would be among the men waiting for introductions. He married Marie Rose who had just turned twenty-eight.

Yvette, the youngest sister was twenty-four. After rejecting two men, she married a surgeon, Francois Gregoire. They also settled in Quebec City. Francois had worked onboard several ships after graduating from the Institute of Surgery in Paris for he'd been recruited by the Navy whose orders gave him no choice.

In the large meeting room at the convent where he spoke to Yvette for the first time, Francois introduced himself,

"I am a surgeon in lower Quebec. I have a house, a horse and some livestock." He paused, looked down at the hat he was holding in his hands. "For eight years I worked on ships where I removed arms and legs. Here, I often do the same, for many men are injured in their work felling trees or building with rocks. Some people lose limbs from gangrene. When I'm not cutting their bodies, I'm pulling teeth." He looked into her face for a reaction, but saw none. She just looked into his eyes. "On the ships I did the work of a dentist every day. If there was no work, I worked as a barber for I am skilled with a razor. I can provide for you well."

If it hadn't been for the slight smile on his face that gave him an air of amusement as he told about his experiences, Yvette might have been put off by such descriptions, but she found herself smiling back, grateful that he'd ended by telling her about his work as a barber.

They too were married and their early years passed uneventfully until one August night, two years after their marriage, the couple was awakened by the sounds of screams and the smell of smoke. Fearing the worst, they ran out of their house in their nightdresses and bare feet and saw that their city was in flames. The fire blazed for two nights as most of the houses were made of wood. More than fifty houses were destroyed.

Later, a law was passed that all future buildings would have walls made of sandstone or limestone. Their house was spared, but they stayed with friends some distance away until they were sure that it would be safe to return.

Andre and Marie Rose were not quite so lucky. Their house was badly damaged. They were away at the time and returned to find that they had no home. They joined Yvette and Francois until the house was rebuilt.

Marie Rose and Yvette both gave birth to daughters within days of each other. Catherine and Etienne made the long trip to Quebec for the christening a month later. It would be the first time that Catherine had seen Andre Gervais since they'd said their goodbyes so long ago in Paris. She'd heard of his marriage to her sister Marie Rose and had not given it much thought. But when she realized that they would be meeting, she could think of nothing else. Anticipating the visit, she glanced in the mirror more often than usual, wondering if the years had been kind to her.

When she entered the Gervais home, she saw Andre coming toward her. She felt a weakness in her knees. He had changed a bit. He looked weary, somehow, yet more worldly. He came to her immediately and clutched both of her hands. At last they were face to face.

"My dear little childhood friend. My dear Catherine, you are lovelier than ever. How good to see you again."

His eye patch gave him a dignified appearance. She introduced Etienne. As the two men stood side by side, though the same age, Etienne appeared younger, stronger, and healthier. She reminded herself of her mother's words: "Love comes after marriage." But when Andre put his arm around her sister's waist, a strange feeling came over Catherine and her throat felt tight.

"I think I need a breath of air and then a little rest. It was a long journey." She remembered the handkerchief that he'd claimed for himself those many years ago, and wondered what had become of it.

By the end of the century, visitors from France would be astonished to see many beautiful three-story stone houses in Lower and Upper Quebec. Excellent stonemasons had come from France and built the large homes in the style of fine Norman architecture. Magnificent cathedrals were built and sculptors were commissioned to adorn the altars of the churches with carved and gilded wood.

The year1675 saw the end of most immigration to Canada. France was fighting what some historians have referred to as the First World War. The country was over-extended militarily and financially. There were no more large investors. The roughly ten thousand settlers were independent of France except for some military support. They had more or less been abandoned by the mother country. Their enemies were the Iroquois and the British who greatly outnumbered them in the colonies of New England. The ten thousand would have to stand alone.

CHAPTER 13

LACHINE

Twelve years had passed since Marie Therese and Charlotte, Catherine's old friends from the Golden Eagle, had settled in Lachine, roughly ten miles from Montreal. Catherine would now have opportunities to see them again.

In 1656, the two women with their large families joined their husbands in the homes that they'd built beneath the shadow of the large stone windmill. Besides the grinding of corn and wheat, it had holes through which to use arms in case of enemy attacks. Compared to Quebec, Lachine was vulnerable geographically, as was the island of Montreal. Its convenience was for the fur trade. There were 75 houses in the village, and 375 inhabitants. The elder children from both families had married, and continued to live in the homes of their parents. Many of the families were related.

Charlotte was living the life she had dreamed of so long ago on the *Golden Eagle*. Marie Therese, who had doubted the possibility of wealth, was living a comfortable life as well. Both had married brothers who were in the fur trade. Francois and Joseph Rivard had the good luck to get the coveted *conge*, a license that allowed them to travel west toward the Great Lakes and to take part in the commerce.

In forty-foot canoes with their guides, *coureurs du bois*, and several

Indians, Joseph and Francois would hunt beaver or trade for pelts along the river, stopping at forts for supplies where small settlements had sprung up.

The European demand for beaver hats was almost insatiable and very profitable. In addition, there were still hopes of discovering the Northwest Passage to China and Japan.

In 1679, one sailing ship, *The Griffon* had made it to the northern part of Lake Michigan under the command of Robert Cavalier de LaSalle, the great explorer. Born in 1643 in Rouen, he was the son of a wealthy merchant, and a scholar of the Jesuits. He came to *Nouvelle-France* with his own agenda. LaSalle sent a message to King Louie XIV requesting another ship to further his explorations.

Charlotte's second son, Pierre, had joined La Salle in the exploration of the Great Lakes, for the feudal lord who granted land in Lachine was greatly admired. He'd been successful as an explorer and in the fur trade and he spoke several Indian languages.

A young Jesuit, Father Hennepin, whom La Salle had convinced to sail with him, kept daily records of their activities and wrote letters for him.

As a young man, LaSalle himself was ordained a Jesuit, but he left the order. He couldn't foresee a life of teaching young boys and was more driven by a sense of adventure, and his own moral compass.

At the time of the building of *The Griffon*, the Indians were amazed that such a large ship could be built, especially after their first impression that the French Beards, as they called them, were disgusting in their poor hygiene, hairy faces and ridiculous clothing. Moreover, the French seemed to lack common sense.

In 1679, LaSalle received permission for the building of the new ship. He sent *The Griffon* from Green Bay to Niagara with a skeleton crew of five, one of whom was Pierre, Charlotte's son. The ship was loaded with sixteen thousand pounds of furs to trade for materials for the building of the new ship.

From the time it began its journey, no sighting of *The Griffon* was ever reported, and neither the ship nor the crew was ever found. Foul play was suspected, and the suspects were many. They included the Ottawas, fur traders, the crew and pilot. Even the Jesuits were suspect. It became the Holy Grail of the Great Lakes.

In 1680, Hennepin and LaSalle were captured by the Sioux and forced to walk with them through miles of forest. After their release they had a difficult journey back to Quebec. Father Hennepin wrote about his experiences, and the book became a best seller in Europe and was translated into several languages. Earlier, he'd also written about the building of *The Griffon*, just six miles from Niagara Falls. He was the first European to describe the falls based on personal observation.

Lachine received its name, China, in mockery for the explorers led by La Salle who were trying to find a passage to Asia. When they returned, unsuccessful in their quest, they were named *Les Chinois*, the Chinese.

The citizens of France complained about the huge sums of money being spent in Canada for sailing ships and soldiers, and these complaints were mounting. They could always be told that it was for exploration or to carry the word of God to the savages, but the driving force was wealth.

Lachine prospered. With wealth pouring in from the fur trade, there was a need for entrepreneurs. After Catherine moved to Montreal, she would occasionally see her old friends from the crossing when she came to Lachine. It had been many years since they'd left Paris and the women were approaching forty.

Her purpose in making the trip was to buy fabrics that came from France for a special dress, or to buy a hat from the haberdashery where she liked the work of a black hatter, a slave who tended a shop there. Her hats suited Catherine best.

One day, while walking along the muddy street watching her every step, she bumped into a young farmer who was carrying vegetables from his wagon. They both apologized and stepped aside for the other, but she was shocked to see before her a young Andre, an Andre without the injured shoulder. She glanced into his clear brown eyes, those eyes reminiscent of her first love, and they went their separate ways.

No way could she nor Andre Gervais have predicted the events that followed his summer on the farm after that long march from New York.

The young woman who'd come to him and shared her blanket long ago had married just weeks after the soldiers departed and her first-born arrived eight months after the wedding. Her husband was delighted that his wife had given birth to a son.

Catherine walked along the street in Lachine where dolls in the fashionable stores, dressed in the latest Parisian styles, provided temptation for the women. Marie Therese and Charlotte succumbed more often than Catherine, and ordered the dresses that were displayed, for their husbands had become wealthy. Catherine sewed her own dresses with the help of her oldest daughter.

After meeting in the shops, or by prior arrangement, Charlotte sometimes invited her friends into her home for tea. There, she spoke a little of her husband's drinking habits. "He drinks much too much, but when he does, he is soon asleep. Then I'm not bothered by him in our bed, except for his loud snoring."

At this point, she laughed at herself in a hearty manner. "Besides, he's often away and I enjoy my life with my family."

Catherine was relieved by this conversation for she prayed for

Charlotte who had suffered so much in her last years in Paris and later from the loss of her seventeen-year-old son who was never found after the disappearance of the *Griffon*.

The decade had been a peaceful one, but tensions were growing. The English, especially the Governor of Albany, stirred up the Iroquois Nation made up of Mohawks, Senecas, Oneidas, and Onondagas, against the French who had made incursions and warfare into Indian territories and pushed them even further westward.

When forty Onondagas, the most honored of the Iroquois arrived as envoys at the site of Fort Frontenac, they were seized, chained, and shipped to France as galley slaves.

In 1687, Governor Denonville and his men ravaged the Seneca lands with a hundred newly arrived, aimless soldiers from the ports of France. The Iroquois, great warriors when fighting guerilla style, had been helpless, asleep in their villages when they were attacked and their families butchered by the French.

Now, the Iroquois would not remain peaceful. At first, small isolated French homesteads were attacked and whole families killed. These attacks increased. There had been signs of war for many years. Palisades surrounded both Montreal and Quebec and French soldiers were billeted in private homes where they were well fed and well dressed. The Lachine residents went on with their daily lives unaware of the extent of the tensions that were brewing between the French soldiers and the Indians.

On the night of August 4, 1689 fifteen hundred Iroquois warriors crossed Lake St. Louis, under cover of a hailstorm, and came within a few feet of the homesteads. They took the village by surprise; set the buildings on fire, killing every person they came upon. There were three forts nearby at Remy, Roland and La Presentation and there were two hundred soldiers three miles from Lachine.

A villager who had escaped the horror reached Fort Remy pleading for help. A few more survivors ran toward the fort with Iroquois in pursuit. When seeing the soldiers, the Indians gave up the chase, but ravaged more houses as they retreated. When the news reached Montreal, a group of over one hundred soldiers and as many inhabitants headed toward the town to defend it, but were called back by orders of Governor Denonville.

General Subercase, who led the group of would-be defenders was furious, but orders directly from Montreal said to stand merely on the defensive and to run no risks of all-out war with the Iroquois.

In Lachine, the warriors took out their full wrath on the families, torturing, killing men, women and children. Some were taken prisoner. Fifty-six houses were burned to the ground and all livestock killed. They stayed in Lachine for several days, ransacking, burning and killing. The screams of the victims pierced the night. They continued burning and pillaging over an area of more than nine miles for several weeks.

When five hundred regulars set out from Fort Roland to attack them, all soldiers were killed with exception of a few who escaped to Fort Remy.

Within moments of the surprise attack, Charlotte and her husband perished in their cabin. She was just clearing the table with her eldest daughter when the door flew open and her husband was set upon first, his head split open by the violent blows of a tomahawk. She attempted to run outside, but was pushed back by warriors and struck several times. A young brave, not wanting to make war on children in spite of the killing frenzy around him, hid her two grandchildren in food barrels as their grandparents were set upon. The other warriors failed to notice as their war whoops blended with the screams of their victims.

The little ones, understanding little but survival leaped out and ran into the woods under the cover of smoke while the Indians set the house on fire and burned the rest of the family alive.

Marie Therese, in a house nearby, lost her eldest son and his entire family. Her husband and several of their children died in the first onslaught, just after he had pushed her out the back door. She and two daughters crawled through their garden on the wet ground under the pumpkin vines and through the cornstalks until reaching the woods. There, they found Charlotte's two little grandchildren and ran with the babes in their arms and their hands over their mouths. Hidden by dense trees, they escaped to the fort. One daughter, seven- year-old Lily, Charlotte's youngest, who'd fallen, was captured, held captive for a time and later repatriated.

Of the three hundred who were there that night, eighty died, forty-two were never found. They were perhaps spread throughout the Iroquois confederacy and tortured for the amusement of the tribes. Men, women and children took part in the torture. The victims were kept alive as long as possible for the amusement of their captors. The women would put hot coals in the mouths of the captives, and the children would use their almost lifeless bodies for target practice with bows and arrows. The screams of the victims mixed with the victory cries of the Indians for days. The remaining survivors who had been left for dead were emotionally scarred for the rest of their lives.

Later, when it was deemed safe to return to the area, bodies and limbs were gathered for they'd been strewn over a large area. It would be two months before the bones were buried and masses said.

CHAPTER 14

1685: Revocation of the Edict of Nantes

All was not well in the Mother Country. In October of 1685, four years before the Lachine Massacre, King Louis XIV, the Sun King, revoked the Edict of Nantes that had protected French Huguenots from discrimination and worse.

The Edict signed by his grandfather, Henry IV, had ended the religious wars since the signing in 1598. There had been almost a hundred years of religious tolerance

Now, Huguenot churches and homes were burned to the ground or pillaged. They were no longer allowed to practice their religion, nor were they allowed to leave the country. Their newborn children had to be baptized by parish priests. The word 'heretics' was heard throughout the land.

Late one night there was a knock at the door of the home of Barbe and Jean in Dieppe. The elderly couple was dozing before the fire when Barbe awakened suddenly. She instinctively turned to her husband and shook his arm.

"Jean, who could be calling at this hour? Please see to the door."

Jean tossed the blanket that he'd placed over his knees, reached for his cane and walked to the door.

In the dim light, he recognized the form of his daughter. "Mary Catherine? Why are you here at this late hour? Who is with you?" His son-in-law, Aleander Langevin, soon appeared beside Mary Catherine. They stepped inside.

"We've come to say goodbye. We are joining other members of our congregation and we're leaving Dieppe. We are leaving France. It's too dangerous here. Oh, dear Papa, perhaps I shan't ever see you again." She ran into the room and reached for her mother, who was walking toward her. Kissing Barbe's hands and face, her tears fell upon her.

Her parents, aware of the hostilities toward the Huguenots, had tried to protect their daughter and her family, and had encouraged them to come back to the Catholic Church, as had many Huguenots to avoid harassment, but to no avail. Jean spoke up, "You will be severely punished if you ever try to return to France."

His daughter replied, "We are being punished every day by staying. We can't tolerate it anymore. Our friends' homes have been burned to the ground and our church is gone. Our decision is made."

At break of day, the Langevin family, consisting of nine people from three generations, left Dieppe and traveled on foot with a small horse-drawn wagon, to the city of Erlangen, Germany. The trip took several weeks. In the first days, they had to travel at dusk or dawn to avoid being found and returned to France where severe punishment awaited them.

Thousands of Huguenots had gone before them. Their closest friends and other members of the Langevin family, more than forty men women and children, had already gone by ship to Charles Town, the southernmost point of English settlement in the colonies. Others had gone to Switzerland, and the north of Africa.

In Erlangen, in Bavaria, they'd been promised housing, land, shops and the benefit of living tax- free. The leaders of Erlangen knew of the skills that the Huguenots would bring and hoped to bolster their own economy with this new population. Yet, the first arrivals found only land. In time, they built their own community with aid from the city fathers who made good on their promises. The citizens of Erlangen resented this and shunned these strange people who spoke a different language, but the clever and industrious Huguenots soon opened shops, built a beautiful church started in 1686 and completed in 1693. Among them were hatters, silkmakers, designers, and silversmiths.

In Dieppe, the departure of the Langevin family was the final blow for Barbe who had now lost her treasured grandchildren and great grandchildren! Only Laurent and his wife remained nearby, and they were childless.

Soon the Langevin elders started a glove making business and one of their sons became a hosiery maker. Their daughter married a whittawer, a maker of saddles, harnesses and padded collars for horses.

In time, many Huguenots returned to France. The Langevin family remained in Germany until several generations later, in 1750, when their descendants would settle in Western Canada.

When called to arms by the British, their sons would fight against the French in the Battle of the Plains of Abraham in 1759.

CHAPTER 15
1690-1720 MONTREAL

Catherine slept fitfully, recalling the Lachine massacre. She'd heard from one person who'd escaped the encampment that some of the seventy prisoners taken that night were burned, roasted and eaten!

Thinking of Charlotte and her husband who'd been hacked to death and perhaps scalped, and the family of Marie Therese and all the others, caused her many sleepless nights. Haunted by the visions of families that had perished when their homes burned to the ground, she developed an overwhelming fear of fire and with good reason, for fire was a constant threat even in times of peace.

When Etienne or one of her sons was adding wood to the fire, she would warn, "Be careful. Watch out for sparks. Don't you see that some of the embers are flying out onto the hearth? Our homes are so close together. The Benoit family died and it's no wonder! When I visited their house their fires were blazing and no one seemed to be vigilant! It's a wonder it didn't reach our house."

As a further caution she insisted that a bucket of sand and a bucket of water be kept by the fire at all times. Her family put up with her constant reminders and followed her suggestions.

As the years passed, her solace came from her grandchildren.

Unlike in France, where children were often considered a nuisance and were often beaten, some of the Canadians learned gentleness toward children from their Indian neighbors. Etienne was a patient father and grandfather, never raising a hand to the children. Among the *habitants*, it was quite a different story. On their small farms and with families often numbering over twenty, the children experienced the brutality of hard work and were just seen as helping hands and mouths to feed.

With her grandchildren once again, Catherine became their teacher and saw to their lessons every day, much as her parents had done for her and her sisters, and she'd done for her own children. She was shocked by the general lack of respect for learning and for books in this new land.

"I don't understand the priests here who have banned so many books. They discourage all reading except for the reading of holy books. I love my church, but I can't agree with this policy. Our lives were enriched because of the literature and poetry that our mother read to us." Etienne wasn't prepared to argue with the clergy nor with his wife, and he solemnly nodded his head in agreement.

The children adored their *Memere* Catherine and even without books she regaled them with stories about her voyage to *Nouvelle-France* and her early years in the cabin and of Etienne hunting, clearing land and living in the wilderness. She told them of a bear that had once startled her at her back door, of bobcats basking in the sun and stretching like large house cats, and of the coyote who brought her pups closer and closer for her to admire. They loved her stories about her Indian friend who taught her to make pemmican. She told them of gathering wild rice in the same bogs where they found the cranberries growing on long vines in the water. She and her grandchildren mixed ground deer meat and cranberries and strung the balls on strings just as Rosebud had taught her.

She used the juice of the cranberry to dye wool from their sheep and taught the children to spin.

With their grandfather *Pepere* Etienne, the children carved wood. He praised their simple efforts when they tried to imitate the songbirds and small animals that he made for them. He whittled the points of goose feathers to make pens and ground ink for their writing lessons. When paper was scarce, he pressed onionskin for their simple books.

The children used charcoal for sketching. But all was not play. The boys and girls had many skills to learn to survive in this land. Planting, harvesting, carpentry, weaving, knitting, sewing and cooking were but of a few of the skills that they were taught from the age of five. No hands were idle. The girls sat at their grandmother's knee knitting mittens while the boys helped their grandfather to stack wood. They attended the school nearby and brought home their penmanship and catechism lessons. They had passages to memorize every night. When the time came to receive the sacraments of Holy Communion and Confirmation, the homework increased and they were kept at school for long rehearsals. As each child entered these rites of passage, there were family celebrations.

Pepere Etienne took them sugaring in the early spring. There was still snow on the ground, and he pulled the little ones on a sled while the older children used snowshoes.

What they most enjoyed was when Etienne tossed hot maple syrup on the snowy ground. The syrup immediately became taffy. Though it stuck to their mittens, they picked it up and couldn't wait to get the delicious candy into their mouths.

Time passed and the children grew. Montreal grew. There were four generations at the table and grandchildren did the serving as their elderly grandparents sat by the iron stove that had replaced their fireplace. Their last two decades in Nouvelle-France were peaceful ones.

After a brief illness, with several family members by her side, Catherine died at the age of eighty-six.

Etienne was now in his nineties. Unable to live without his wife with her eyes the color of a bluebird or a crisp, blue September sky, he followed her into eternal peace. The year was 1720. Behind them, they left a legacy of eighty-six grandchildren and forty-three great grandchildren.

Catherine had fulfilled the desire of King Louie X1V and done her duty as a Daughter of the King.

CHAPTER 16
THE GREAT PEACE

In 1701, the French met with thirty-nine leaders of the Indian nations and signed a peace treaty. The Iroquois had decided to compromise. They had been devastated by war and disease, trade had moved to New England and the demand for furs had fallen.

In the past, peace treaties signed between the Great Indian Nations had failed, but this time there would be careful negotiations, for their survival depended on it. More than a thousand delegates made their way to Montreal. With them was the greatest ally of the French, the Huron Chief Kondiaronk.

He addressed the assembly. "We are ill. We have walked over bodies to get here." He was ill himself, but he spoke for hours. "We spread the soft white feathery down of the globe thistle as seats for you. We place you upon those seats beneath the shade of the spreading branches of the Tree of Peace."

The Indians wanted the return of prisoners who had been taken as slaves.

After much discussion and banquets, the Iroquois agreed to be neutral between the French and English colonies and a treaty was signed. The French agreed to arbitrate during conflicts between tribes.

Soon after, the great Huron Chief died of influenza at the age of fifty-two. He was given an elaborate funeral, as elaborate as that of Samuel Champlain, first as an Iroquois in a ritual called 'covering the dead.'

During this ritual, a procession of sixty men led by Chabert de Joncaire with the Seneca Chief Tonatakout at the end of the line, made a circle around the body. There were chants for several hours and then the chanter walked around the circle wiping the tears of the mourners. In a gesture where he appeared to force each man's mouth open, he then gave him a drink of sweet liquid medicine to revive his spirits, urging the warriors to 'emerge from darkness to the light of peace.'

When that ceremony ended, the coffin was covered with flowers, a sword and a plumed hat. French officers carried it to Notre Dame Church in Montreal, for the chief was a convert to Catholicism. His relatives were directly behind the coffin, followed by chiefs of the tribes in attendance, the Governor of Montreal and his wife, and the entire corps of French officers. The war leaders fired a salute at the grave. The inscription at his grave read 'Here lies The Muskrat. Chief of the Hurons."

Commerce resumed and the people lived without fear for the most part, though there were occasional skirmishes. There was more exploration of the Great Lakes, and the city of Detroit was founded.

In the nineteenth century, the historian Francis Parkman wrote:

"Spanish civilization crushed the Indian; English civilization scorned and neglected him; French civilization embraced and cherished him."

Five decades later, in the 1750s everything would change for the French and the Indians.

CHAPTER 17
MONTREAL IS BURNING-1734

Marie Elizabeth, Catherine's eldest daughter, now almost seventy, had reason to recall her mother's fear of fire when on Saturday, April 10, 1734 Montreal experienced a fire that destroyed the center of the city. Amazingly, everyone survived.

Later Marie Elizabeth recounted the events of that evening to her first son, Pierre, who'd returned from his business in Lachine.

"Around seven o'clock we had finished our evening meal. That's when the first cry of 'fire' was heard. Everyone rushed to the streets or to their windows. We saw that the fire was spreading rapidly! People tried to put it out with buckets of water, but to no avail. How fortunate we were that our house survived. If the wind hadn't changed direction, our street would have been next."

The next day, she and several members of her family went to the aid of the Sisters at the site of the *Hotel Dieu*, their hospital that had burned to the ground.

Carrying food, water and blankets, they found the nuns in the center of the garden, huddled in the small Chapel of the Most Holy Virgin. The remains of their hospital smoldered and the air was thick with smoke.

The first person that Marie Elizabeth saw was Sister Veronique, whom she knew. The Sister wept as she recounted their ordeal. "We tried to contain the fire when it started on the side of the church, but fire on the other side had spread to our roof. Two Sisters were trying to salvage goods from the dormitory and refused to leave. When the roof collapsed, they heard people crying to them to get out. Only by running down a flaming staircase were they able to make it to safety.

It was such a cold evening. We all found ourselves in mud up to our knees."

Most of the Sisters refused food. One of them said, "The good seminary fathers brought us bread and cheese, but we are too distraught to eat, but maybe a little water?" Marie Elizabeth passed the bottle to her and after taking a few sips, the Sister quickly passed it to others who were huddled in the small space.

Later, the citizens assessed the damage. Their hospital and forty -six houses would have to be rebuilt. In this city with a population of slightly more than two thousand, people knew each other and came to the aid of the needy. Marie Elizabeth gave shelter to seven extra people in her house.

An angry group gathered at the ruins of the Hospital *Hotel Dieu*. An Indian slave girl who was around ten said she'd seen Marie Joseph Angelique carrying a coal hod just before the fire broke out.

Marie Elizabeth's younger son, Henri Demers, came in with the latest news. "Did you hear that they have arrested Angelique? They are sure that she set the fire. It seems strange because some people said that she was the one who ran from house to house crying fire and earlier was trying to put it out. Hearing her, they'd run out of their houses."

"Do you mean the slave woman who belongs to the Widow Francheville? I can't believe that. Why would she do that? Would she have destroyed her own home?" "Someone said that she was going to be sold," he added.

His mother continued, "The poor thing has had so much tragedy. First she lost her twins, who died at the age of one, and then her three-year-old daughter just days later. I knew the children's father, Jacques Cesar, a slave from Madagascar."

Her son said, "All I know is what I heard at the meeting if you could call it that. Everyone was shouting and someone said that last year, she ran away with her lover, an indentured servant, Claude Thibeault. Before leaving with him, she'd set a fire to distract people from searching for her. They didn't get very far and the fire she'd started didn't amount to anything. Her owner took her back without any consequences. They were trying to run away to the colonies." He shook his head and continued, "Claude Thibeault is nowhere to be found."

Marie Elizabeth tried to take it all in. "What will become of her?"

"I don't know. Her trial will be held next week. People were screaming that she should have her hands cut off and that she should be burned alive." Every day, there was more news of the trial. Everyone was talking about it and of nothing else.

They learned that Marie Joseph Angelique was born in Portugal and sold to an Englishman who later sold her to *Monsieur* Poulin de Francheville when she was twenty-four. When he died, she belonged to his widow who was away on business at the time of the second fire.

After being tortured for days, she confessed to the crime. Finally, her sentence was set. It was reduced to hanging.

She was paraded through the streets, hanged, and then burned. Her ashes were scattered throughout the village.

Marie Elizabeth remained in her house that day. The roar of the crowd could be heard from her windows. Her thoughts were in the past, for she had delivered Marie Angelique's children.

"I just remember her as a young woman giving birth. How could she have done such a thing?"

Her husband said, "How much better it would have been if she had died with them, but it wasn't the will of God."

CHAPTER 18
SMALLPOX

Angelique's children had died of smallpox. Little did she or anyone else know that there was an inoculation to prevent the dreaded disease. Europeans and people of North America knew little about diseases in general. They were still relying on religious books written in the second century. The Catholic Church forbade autopsies and the crime for performing them was death.

Years later, Cotton Mather, a Boston clergyman, would stem the smallpox epidemics. He had read a 1714 article by a Turkish doctor about inoculation. Most Royal courts had Jews or Moslems as doctors for they were trained in Arabian medical schools that were greatly advanced.

In 1721 there was a smallpox epidemic in Boston, of the three hundred who'd been inoculated six of them died, but the rest didn't get the disease. British and French doctors began inoculating the public. The information spread to Canada.

There were still other diseases to fear. There was scarlet fever for which there was no cure, and its symptoms were unknown until it was too late for some. From 1751 to 1753 a diphtheria epidemic ravaged the country. The disease struck quickly and terrorized the population. People boiled their clothes outside and the clothes of the sick were burned. After tending to the ill, a person would take a hot bath and change into clean clothes. Morticians refused to handle the bodies. This epidemic was followed by typhus, thought to be spread by lice. When it was suspected that lice favored linens, and that wool and cotton seemed less hospitable to them, it temporarily put an end to the raising of flax.

BOOK 2
LA GUERRE DE LA CONQUEST
THE WAR OF THE CONQUEST

CHAPTER 1
BAPTISTE PRIVATEER OR NAVAL HERO

The year was 1758. Charles Demers was talking with his young son, Nicholas, and his nephew, Joseph. They were driving along the King's Highway that followed the Saint Lawrence River, linking Quebec, Trois Riviers and Montreal. Lavaltrie, a small town, was their home east of Montreal.

It was a fine spring day and the three sat up front in their small wagon, pulled by their horse "Tit Belle." The boys always enjoyed the trip to Montreal for supplies and Charles relied on Joseph who was fifteen and strong enough to load the goods. The city was the center of the fur trade and for outfitting expeditions. It attracted many retail customers. Everything was scarce in Quebec and Trois Rivieres.

Charles planned to buy everyday supplies including tea, coffee, and sugar. With winter coming he hoped to purchase buffalo robes for their horse drawn sleighs and carriages, and furs for his wife, as well as new hats for the family.

These days, with so much of the fur trade going to Europe, the prices were probably better in France.

Usually, Charles would have made this trip by boat, but the

British Navy had their ships spread along a hundred miles of the St. Lawrence.

In spite of the length of the journey by wagon, Charles was eager to spend the nights on farms along the way. Even if they didn't know the farmer, they were sure to be received with great hospitality and enthusiasm. After purchasing goods and visiting family, they would return to Lavaltrie in two weeks.

The *Chemin du Roy*, the longest road in North America, was one hundred and fifty miles long and about twenty -five feet wide. One could travel from Quebec City to Montreal in about five days. The highway was started in 1706. Each of the landowners along the route was responsible for its maintenance. It was a community chore under the supervision of the local militia who took orders from a parish priest or lord.

As the travelers approached Montreal, they would have to take a ferry or a barge to reach the Island of Montreal. Ferries, barges, and canoes also were maintained by the population who dwelt near these streams and rivers.

The boys were amusing themselves by playing a game called button whizzing. It involved spinning a button on a length of twine.

Immersed in his own thoughts, and addressing no one in particular, Charles muttered, "We are fighting the British now in the forts along the New York border and they have been the enemies of France for so long. Let us hope that our generals continue to keep them away from Quebec."

The boys stopped their game and looked toward him with interest.

"Ah, my boys. It is the desire of the British to control all of North America, but even the Americans are beginning to rebel against them in the colonies.

Let me tell you about your cousin, Jean Baptiste. We could use a few men like him now." He settled into his storytelling mode.

"This happened many decades ago and I want you to decide if this relative of yours was a pirate, as the British called him, or a hero."

Hearing the word 'pirate' the boys leaned forward in anticipation.

"In 1692, during just six months he captured nine English vessels; can you imagine? Some were right within sight of the citizens of Boston.

Well, in 1694, he captured ten vessels. Frontenac, the Governor of New France was so impressed with him that he sent him to Paris so he might tell of his adventures to the Minister of Marine. His real name was Pierre Maisonnat, but he was called Jean Baptiste or Baptiste or even Baptiste the Pirate. That was more than sixty years ago. My father remembered the stories that he heard from his father."

Little Nicholas was especially pleased, for this was the only time that his father spoke directly to him except for reminding him of chores. "Go on, Papa. Tell us the story." His father continued. "In 1694 he was given his own ship, *La Bonne*, flying the French flags and equipped with French cannon. The French government hired him to protect the fishing grounds within sight of Acadian lands. Of course, the British set out to capture him. They brought him to Boston in shackles where the plan was to hang him, but a new war broke out that made him a political prisoner under the rules of war. He was kept a prisoner on Castle Island in Boston until 1706.

The French wanted Jean Baptiste released and the Abenaki Indians were tired of the settlers taking their lands as they moved westward. This led to a horrible event. It was called the Deerfield massacre.

I am sorry to say that the Canadians have done some terrible things, but most of the people in Quebec were just busy trying to live, taking care of their families and working their farms.

At that time, Deerfield was the last frontier of the colonies. The attack by three hundred French and Indians was as bloody as the Lachine massacre. The people of Deerfield were equally unsuspecting.

John Williams, their first pastor and a famous preacher, was sought out in retribution for the arrest of Jean Baptiste.

Women and children were tomahawked, including the preacher's two youngest children and his slave, a black woman named Parthena. The town was looted and houses and barns were burned. Small streams that flowed through the town were red with blood."

Nicholas sat silently the whole time that his father spoke and when his father paused to reach for bread, with butter and maple sugar that his wife had packed for them, Nicholas said, "Go on, father. What happened then?" Nicholas ignored the bread in his hand, but his cousin Joseph took it eagerly. A growing boy, he could listen and eat at the same time.

"They took one hundred and twelve people captive and left forty-eight dead. It took them seven weeks to walk to Montreal in three feet of snow. You can imagine that some of them died, and some of the wounded that couldn't keep up were killed, including the wife of John Williams. She had just given birth and was very weak. Her husband survived along with sixty of the captives who were eventually released.

Five of John Williams' children were among the captives. The Indians treated them with tenderness. Now, that is something very interesting. Sometimes, the Indians adopted people to replace members of their tribes who had died of illness, or who'd been killed in battle. When that happened, the adopted members were treated as though they were indeed members of the tribe. Perhaps that's what happened with the Williams children.

They would hold an elaborate ceremony where the dead person would be mourned and it would end with a joyful ceremony that brought the new person into the tribe. It's strange isn't it how such contradictions can exist, but it is so.

In 1706, Jean Baptiste was exchanged for the famous preacher. The raid was successful, but what a price was paid. What a price." His father shook his head and paused.

"John Williams wrote a book about his experience and of his young daughter, who married an Indian man and chose to remain with the Indians for her whole life. The book was entitled, "The Redeemed Captive Returning to Zion." Sometimes, the young woman and her husband would visit her parents in Mansfield, Connecticut, but the couple always returned to their tribe. Maybe life with Indians was easier than life with those Puritans! What do you say, my son? Would you prefer the life of a young man hunting and canoeing on our beautiful rivers and becoming a brave or being the son of one of those ministers and spending every day in a cold, bare church?"

Without hesitation, Nicholas answered, "A brave, Papa, but with our friends the Mohawks and the Hurons, not the Iroquois. What happened to Baptiste after that?"

Joseph who'd been silent until this time said, "I wouldn't want to live the way the Indians live now. They live like the *habitants*, only poorer. They plant their small gardens. Maybe I would have liked it long ago when the braves hunted and fished without us, and *Huronia* was their home."

"Papa, tell us more about Baptiste!" insisted Nicholas.

"Well, later, he was Port Captain in Nova Scotia at Beaubassin. It was the richest settlement in Nova Scotia until the British raided it twice with their allies the Iroquois. Once was in retribution for Deerfield. That's how war is. People just aren't willing to forget.

When the Treaty of Utrecht obliged the French to leave Newfoundland and Acadia, those poor farmers were put on ships with just what they were wearing. Families were separated and dropped off all along the east coast, in Louisiana, and even in the Caribbean.

There are so many stories about Baptiste. Toward the end of his career, he led land troops against the British. He was clever all right, on land and sea. He was clever in his private life, too. He had many wives. It is said that he had wives in France, Holland, Acadia, and Quebec. The last family was wise to him and they interrupted his marriage to their young daughter. Some of these stories are true, but who knows?"

A long silence followed and the two boys, leaning into each other, slept peacefully for the rest of the journey. Charles drove along the flat road with farms to the right and the beautiful river to his left. Smoking his pipe, he enjoyed the spring sun, and his view of the newly planted fields. The rows of corn, potatoes and pumpkin resembled a patchwork quilt.

Anyone witnessing "Tit Belle" prancing along, would have found the scene bucolic, but in the back of his mind, Charles was worrying about the future of his homeland. The British presence in the colonies had reached over a million, and as the road followed the river, their ships were in plain sight.

Ah, Jean Baptiste. We need your strategy.

His thoughts turned to an event that occurred just four years earlier in May of 1754. Fourteen French emissaries on a diplomatic mission were traveling through Western Pennsylvania. There, they were met by a party of British soldiers and Indians, under the command of a young sergeant named George Washington. When his scouts sounded the alarm that the French were nearby, Washington ordered his men to shoot. The French waved white handkerchiefs and tried to make themselves understood but to no avail. His men opened fire. Before Washington's very eyes, the Indians went on to scalp and kill the wounded. The Half King, the Indian leader, proudly took the scalps.

Both the French and the English paid their Indian allies scalp

PATRICE DEMERS KANEDA

fees, so the warriors were eager to get as many scalps as they could. The victims almost always died.

How can we avoid war now? Charles mused. Like the innocent people of Deerfield and the innocent people of Lachine, is there a chance that we too will be killed in our beds or in our homes? And why? For political reasons that we know little about. May God protect us.

Charles' concerns were justified, for recently, British forces had captured Fort Frontenac on Lake Ontario, and Fort Ticonderoga between Lake Champlain and Lake George. Earlier, the French had had some victories, but the tide was turning.

Glancing at the innocent boys, Charles slowed *Tit Belle* a bit and savored the present calm. He rested his eyes on the view before him of wheat fields, windmills, and farms all along the beautiful river. Sunset was approaching. The river shimmered with its reflection. He'd have to think about stopping soon.

After a good night's sleep and a hearty breakfast at the Mathieu farm, where they found a welcome, the little group looked forward to arriving in Montreal.

They drove for hours and at dusk they reached the ferry crossing. It was a lovely sight. To the east and west, there were valleys and fields as far as the eye could see, and the three peaks of *Mont Royal* to the north. Montreal or *Ville Marie,* as it still was sometimes called, was surrounded by a parapet four feet high, and a moat-like ditch that was eight feet deep.

They drove off the ferry ramp toward the entrance of the Recollet Fathers, those mendicants who served the poor, and passed their convent and gardens. When they reached the Governor General's Palace, and the War Office, the little group saw a city bustling with tradesmen with horse drawn wagons. There were rows of wooden and stone houses, one or two stories high.

"Look at the dogcarts, Uncle Charles." The boys were amused by the dogcarts delivering milk and meat. Some with a small child alongside, carried water from the river.

Montreal was the military heart of Canada and its social center as well. A little piece of Versailles gaiety and frivolity went on here with members of the Old World and the New. There were countless parties and balls. Charles and the boys spent several days with his cousin, Francine Papin. She worked as a servant in the grand house where General Montcalm was staying .

"I've attended some of the parties," she said. "There is dancing and conversation. I heard the general say that he was glad to get away from Quebec and the gambling that goes on there. I also had to unpack the goods he received from his wife. There was English lavender, olives, anchovies, capers and bolts of damask. I heard him complain that half of what was sent by her was taken when a British ship captured 'La Superbe.' The French are living royally here in Montreal. We ordinary citizens know little of it."

Charles, Nicholas and Joseph returned to Lavaltrie with a wagonload of goods and stories about Montreal life for his wife. They would all be hearing more about the General Montcalm.

CHAPTER 2
THE END OF THE FRENCH REGIME, 1759

In June of 1759 a flotilla of English warships sailed up the St. Lawrence River to lay siege to Quebec City. Charles Demers and his wife, Francoise, great-granddaughter of Catherine and Etienne, were walking toward the pier outside their manor house with Nicholas on that day in Lavaltrie.

They were on their way to deliver linen textiles that Francoise had woven with her daughters in exchange for more flax from a neighboring family who received flax, smoked meats, and wool as payment from the *habitants* who worked their land.

As the trio approached the river, they saw many small boats as usual. Nicholas noticed Etienne Gregoire sailing a skiff toward their dock. "Papa, Monsieur Gregoire is waving. He's calling to you."

As he came closer, he screamed his message:

"There are so many warships heading toward Quebec City. I can't believe it. We are doomed. Go back. Warn the others. Ring the church bells to call the militia."

The family ran toward the village. "Nicholas, you run to the

church and tell Father Gervais to ring the bells. We'll tell the neighbors to be prepared."They had been doing battle with the British for
years. Earlier, the French had several victories but the British gained
the upper hand in 1758. If they couldn't defeat France in Europe,
they would do it in North America and split *Nouvelle-France* in half.

For the past year, the *Canadiens* had been aware of the British
Navy's presence. They had looked on with worry, for a quarter of
that navy was spread out for a hundred miles along the St. Lawrence.
Twenty- two ships, twenty-seven frigates and eighty transport vessels held nine thousand soldiers and eighteen thousand sailors. They
had interfered with trade in recent months, but there had been little
movement.

In July, at nine o'clock in the evening, the British fired rockets
into Quebec City and burned several houses. Terrorized, the citizens
ran from their homes, praying and screaming. Many grabbed a few
possessions and ran to join relatives in the countryside. The British
continued bombarding a nearly deserted city and hoped to starve
out the remaining citizens.

The war raged on. It was known as The Seven Years War by the
British, and the French and Indian War by the American Colonists,
but the French called it *La Guerre de la Conquete*, The War of the
Conquest.

CHAPTER 3
THE MARQUIS DE MONTCALM

General Montcalm wrote, "The colony is lost. If peace doesn't come, I see nothing that could save it." The French were out-numbered. Their troops were made up of volunteer militia and Indians. The British Navy was the largest in the world. Montcalm begged for more troops from France but none came.

Earlier, in a letter to his mother after his triumph in Ticonderoga, the Marquis de Montcalm wrote, "Never was a general in a more critical position than I was: God has delivered me; his be the praise! He gives me health, though I am worn out with labor fatigue, and miserable dissensions that have determined me to ask for my recall. Heaven grant that I may get it!"

He was highly respected by the militia and by his friends the Indians, but his relationship with Governor Vaudreuil, the Governor of Montreal, was contentious. The governor doubted Montcalm's abilities to lead and wrote to France to ask that he be recalled. Nothing would have pleased Montcalm more, but it didn't happen.

The general had inherited the title of Marquis from his father, along with a lot of debts. Like many aristocrats who had come to Nouvelle-France, he hoped that he could recover financially here.

Two envoys sailed to France, just before ice sealed the harbor. They eluded British ships and arrived at Versailles where they pleaded their case for aid.

"We are vastly outnumbered by the British, the colony needs troops, arms and food."

France had suffered many defeats in Europe. Her navy was crippled and finances depleted. All that Montcalm and his officers would receive for their earlier victories, and their triumph at Fort Ticonderoga, were honors and promotions.

The French Colonel Minister Berryer replied to the appeals of the envoys by saying, "Eh, Monsieur, when the house is on fire one cannot occupy one's self with the stable."

The envoys returned to Quebec in spring with the sad news that little help would be forthcoming. There was a personal message for Montcalm as well. One of his daughters had died. The messenger did not know which of his two daughters it was.

Montcalm had already amassed his troops along the north shore and hoped that winter would defeat the British. Quebec was heavily fortified and sat on top of a cliff, but the south shore was unprotected.

In a desperate effort, the French launched eighty ships chained together. The ships were filled with explosives in hopes of destroying those of the British, but their attempt failed. In spite of a fire a mile wide, little damage was done to the enemy's ships.

CHAPTER 4
THE BATTLE OF THE PLAINS OF ABRAHAM
SEPTEMBER 13TH, 1759

That summer, the British bombarded Quebec without mercy for nine weeks from morning 'til night. Ships carrying food and supplies for the Colony couldn't pass through the armada of thirty-nine ships and fourteen thousand soldiers.

Early one morning, British soldiers made their way up to the Plains of Abraham in Upper Quebec. No one suspected that they would disembark so close to the city. This was the defining moment. It was September of 1759, and both the young English General James Wolfe and brilliant French General Montcalm were mortally wounded on the same day in a fierce battle that lasted for one hour.

Wolfe had ordered his men to load two balls in their muskets before moving up the hill. The French, led by Montcalm, made their way down the hill and fired, but the order was given too early and from too great a distance. They marched closer. Wolfe, the British General, ordered his men to fire, and a mile wide burst of fire reduced the French soldiers, followed by a second volley that decimated them.

French Huguenots who had migrated from Germany to the area west of Quebec were among the British troops.

Then the fierce Scottish Highlanders advanced.

Though they continued to fire shots from the woods, the French were defeated.

A young nun, Marie de la Visitation risked her life tending the wounded in the field. Francoise Demers and some of the women who'd returned to the city hurried to the Quebec General Hospital when they heard of the large number of casualties from both sides that had been taken there. When Francoise reached the bedside of young Joseph Trahan, a neighbor, he grabbed her sleeve and spoke hysterically of the battle, his eyes ablaze.

"We were thousands of young men in elaborate uniforms, hungry, tired from months of battles and lack of supplies on both sides, but still we marched to face the enemy. First, we fired following General Montcalm's order, but we were too far from their line. We walked toward the British until we were looking into their faces. Suddenly, they fired. Our men fell to their knees and the British fired again. That was the end for us. Soon we were fighting man to man. I crawled over bodies to reach the top of the hill, so many bodies. Men were screaming. The loyal Indians who fought with us now lay among the dead. I was glad to be alive and determined to get away from the madness. Suddenly, we heard bagpipes and the Scottish Highlanders came toward us with their swords that could cut a man in two. And yes, they used them. My arm lies somewhere among the fallen. Now I have seen hell."

Releasing Francoise, he clutched the bloody rags that covered the stump of his right arm and wept. She held a dipper to his lips with fresh water and moved on among the men.

Francoise overheard a group of wounded soldiers saying that there were French speakers in British uniforms who fired upon them. These were Huguenots from the western part of Canada that was under British rule. She had heard of Huguenots settling in the west. Among them were descendants of Marie Catherine Demers and her husband, Alexander, who had walked to Erlangen, Germany so long ago.

General Montcalm was among the wounded. Shot in the abdomen, he asked his surgeon how long he had to live and the surgeon replied, "Not many hours my general."

"I'm glad," replied Montcalm. "I don't want to live to see the surrender of Quebec."

Two of his officers approached him for further orders.

"I shall give no more orders. I have more important matters to attend to."

He died at midnight, alone with the Bishop of Quebec, who attended to his final request. Montcalm was buried in a cavity of earth formed by the bursting of a bombshell. He died for his country and that country was France. He was forty-six years old.

Since his arrival in Montreal in 1776, Montcalm had fought valiantly and had proven to be a gifted strategist. Among his greatest victories was the Battle of Carillon in 1758 where, with four thousand troops, he defeated the British Army of more than sixteen thousand.

Yet, his mistake in timing contributed greatly to the loss of this battle on The Plains of Abraham.

The British General, James Wolfe, had a short career as a regimental officer and commanded a well-trained army. Luck figured greatly in this last battle and his order to load the muskets with two shells led to victory. He lost over fourteen hundred men and the French lost more. Wolfe died within hours of the battle. First, shot in the hand, he continued to move up the hill. Then, he was shot in the groin and in the chest. His men moved him to the rear. He heard someone shout, "See them run!"

"Who?" he asked.

"The French," the man answered.

"Follow our enemies," he ordered. "Don't let them retreat."

Minutes later, General Wolfe died.

Both officers would be romanticized in the future because of the drama of their final combat and their deaths within hours of each other on the Plains of Abraham.

One week later, the Governor of Quebec surrendered his city to the British.

Six months later, sixteen thousand men attacked Montreal, but the French would continue to fight and would not surrender for another year.

CHAPTER 5
THE BATTLES CONTINUE
THE SURRENDER OF MONTREAL

General Francois Gaston de Levy replaced Montcalm. With four thousand soldiers he tried to retake Quebec in April of 1760, but their cannon bogged down in wet snow. They resorted to hand to hand combat. A windmill changed hands five times and it appeared that the French had won. Both sides were awaiting reinforcements. At last a warship arrived, but it flew no flag. Soon, it was evident that it carried British troops. The French retreated to Montreal and six months later, seventeen thousand British troops surrounded them, forcing their surrender.

After the French surrender, the great Ojibwa Chief Pontiac made a proclamation to the British. "We are not your slaves. Though you have defeated the French, we are still at war." Pontiac called for total annihilation of the British. "There is no other way. The English are seeking our ruin."

In the past, the tribes had used their relations with the British and French as bargaining chips, the Iroquois supporting the British and the Hurons, the French. But now there would be no such advantage.

The Indian nations lost an ally when the French lost control of

Canada. From the beginning, Europeans had exploited the rivalry that already existed between Indian nations, but with the French, great alliances had been formed and both sides benefited. They were together as allies and in trade.

The British, especially General Amherst, wanted nothing less than to annihilate the Indians. In his letters, he referred to them as vermin and mentioned his desire to wipe them from the earth. It is even thought that it was his plan to have blankets infected with typhus distributed to them.

They, the Indian nations, along with the remaining French, would be the disenfranchised.

The Treaty of Paris was signed on February of 1763, giving the French eighteen months to return to France. It read, *"The French Inhabitants, or others who had been subjects of the Most Christian King in Canada, may retire with all safety and freedom wherever they shall think proper, and may sell their estates, provided it be to the subjects of his Britannick Majesty, and bring away their effects as well as their persons, without being restrained in their emigration, under any pretence whatsoever, except that of debts or of criminal prosecutions. The term limited for this emigration shall be fixed to the space of eighteen months, to be computed from the day of the exchange of the ratification of the present treaty.*

One important concession was made.

His Britannick Majesty will give the most precise and most effectual orders, that his new Roman Catholic subjects may profess the worship of their religion according to the rites of the Romish church as far as the laws of Great Britain permit.

From that time on, the Catholic Church gained even more power in French Canada. Many families returned to France, but things were not going well in that country. Inflation was rampant and there were reports of people starving in Normandy and of rogue soldiers stealing and pillaging from the farmers.

The royal coffers were almost empty. France had been at war all over the globe. From the date of the signing of the treaty in 1763 there would be no more immigration from France. No longer was she a major power in the Americas, for all claim to land east of the Mississippi River was lost including some West Indian Islands.

Under the flag of their old enemies, the French Canadians banded together.

The Demers family met with the Gauthiers, the Gregoires, the Casaubons, the Pelletier's and the Gervais family as soon the news of the signing reached them.

Gathered around the large family table in the Gregoire house, Charles was the first to speak. Looking around at his neighbors' sullen and exhausted faces, he said,

"There is no way that we intend to leave here, I don't know about the rest of you. I am *Canadien*. My family worked for more than a hundred years for what we have now. This is our home. Though General Wolfe and his bombardment have destroyed the house that my father built, I am determined to rebuild it, and when I finish I will help you and our neighbors to rebuild theirs."

In addition to the houses that were destroyed in the city, more than forty farms were burned to the ground in the surrounding countryside. Devastation was everywhere.

Charles, still unbeaten, had lost more than his family home, for just months earlier, his three youngest sisters had drowned while sailing a small boat in the St. Lawrence. A sudden storm had come up and capsized the skiff. Their cries for help were heard from shore, but by the time a rowboat set out to rescue them, they were nowhere in sight. Their bodies washed ashore a few days later and they were buried in the cemetery beside the graves of their two brothers who'd died in infancy.

Red-faced with emotion, stout Mr. Gervais stood and shouted, "We are ten thousand souls. They will never rule us." Every head of household that was present that night voiced the same opinion. Their wives agreed. Little did they know what courage and determination would be demanded of them.

During the siege, they had suffered extreme food shortages, forcing them to eat most of their horses and cattle. They had subsisted mostly on salted cod, eel and meager rations from the King. A barrel of flour cost two hundred francs.

It was hard to watch the flurry of sales of furnishings, land and houses, and even harder to bid goodbye to friends who did decide to leave, but those remaining were determined to keep their language and their faith even under British domination.

Francoise who was usually quiet around men voiced her opinion in her soft voice. "Our very own Jesuit historian, Charlevoix, said that there were more French nobles here than in any other colony, for the sons of the nobility were among the first to arrive as army officers. Their children and grandchildren are large landowners. Will any of their families remain here now? The economic and political climates in France are moving in a very uncertain direction. They would be fools to leave here even under our dire circumstances. We need capable people to survive."

Mr. Gervais shook his head in desolation, shaking his jowls mightily. "I've seen offices closing and houses for sale. I'm afraid we are losing our most talented people.

First, the regular French soldiers were sent back to France on British ships and forbidden to return. Some deserted to remain with their Canadian wives. Merchants and *noblesse* left in such numbers that the British were hard put to supply the needed numbers of ships.

One ship, *Auguste*, carrying soldiers, ladies, and merchants, left in late autumn and encountered a violent storm that ultimately caused the ship to run aground and split in half. A hundred and fourteen corpses floated near the shore, off the coast of Cape Breton. Friendly Indians came to the aid of the survivors.

They gave them snowshoes and helped them to reach Quebec by winter.

The remaining French peasants and colonists were left in despair. They associated only with each other. They refused to learn English. The French clergy encouraged this resistance. "He who keeps the language, keeps the faith."

After the signing of the Treaty of Paris, a policy was implemented preventing Catholics from holding office and forbidding the recruitment of priests and brothers to teach in the schools and universities. That resulted in the closing of the schools. The law was rescinded two years later, and the French-Catholic schools reopened. They kept their language and their faith.

The schools trained good Catholics but taught few skills. The Church gained power that made it as repressive as the conquering nation. The Jesuits heard confession from everyone in their flock and visited the households unannounced. What better way to gain power.

These ten thousand souls, the original Canadians, would become one of the most homogeneous groups ever known.

CHAPTER 6

AFTER THE WAR OF THE CONQUEST

"Thirty want to rule ten thousand!" Andre Gide, 1763

Elizabeth Demers hurried up the stairs from Lower Quebec past the family house that had been destroyed in the bombardments. It was one of 180 fine houses lost in a few days when the British used all their weaponry to conquer the city. She thought of Uncle Jean who had built the house, and how he'd provided for the family. They'd continued to occupy it for fifty years after his death, but now...

Elizabeth was the granddaughter of Catherine and Etienne and the wife of Charles Demers, Sr. Elizabeth learned much from her mother-in-law, her *belle mere*, who was a mid-wife, as was her mother before her, who had delivered Catherine's children in Montreal.

She glanced back at the ruins of the house, raising her handkerchief to her mouth to avoid the dust as the workers cut stone to build the foundation. Eager to reach the young woman in need of her ministrations, she walked hurriedly after leaving the stairs and brushed the dust from the sleeves of her black dress.

She was on her way to the home of a British woman who had given birth the day before. Whigs were coming to Quebec now that it was under British rule for they feared the animosity of their colonial neighbors in New England where rebellion was in the air.

It was rare for a Quebecois to enter the home of an English person. Elizabeth couldn't refuse when she received word that Mrs. Barrows had been in labor for hours and was near exhaustion when suddenly, her labor had stopped.

Yesterday, when she'd walked into the British woman's home with her Huron servant, Leonore, Elizabeth was shocked to find how cold it was. She ordered him to add wood to the fire and lots of it.

"Go quickly to the woodpile and bring in as much dry wood as you can stack here. A home without heat lacks heart. I don't understand why this poor woman is alone. Doesn't she have any friends or neighbors? I don't know when they arrived here in Quebec City, but they certainly didn't choose a good time to do so."

She had heard that the British and Americans preferred to keep their homes cool but she couldn't understand it. French houses were always warm. It was early November. She couldn't deliver a baby with cold hands and wouldn't want to bring it into such an inhospitable world.

Accustomed to having several women to assist her, this time she'd have to make do with Leonore. At least he followed directions well. He was already warming blankets by the fire. It was the woman's first birth and she was frightened but Elizabeth soon put her at ease with her calm manner and rubbed her belly with a warm mixture of oils that included mugwort and tansy. Neither spoke the other's language. Words were not necessary in this world of women.

Supporting her on one side by leaning into her and holding her arm tightly, Elizabeth walked the tall, light-haired woman back and forth in the small room. Her hair was plastered to her scalp, she was sweating so. The woman was slight except for her huge belly. It had dropped, a sign that the baby was ready to be born. She walked awkwardly, clinging to Elizabeth who was much shorter than she. Soon, her labor started again.

Elizabeth sat by the young woman's bedside and knitted as she waited for more contractions. By now, Leonore had found two women in the neighborhood who agreed to assist her. They were accustomed to birthing babies. Fortunately, the delivery went smoothly and, as usual, the infant was born in Elizabeth's lap. When she left, the new mother was holding a son in her arms and the two neighbors remained to care for them.

Today, she returned alone to the English family, and when she reached the house in Upper Quebec, Elizabeth knocked lightly at the door. The woman's husband opened it, nodded his head in greeting and said, "*Bonjour*," perhaps one of the few French words that he had learned since his arrival. She was glad to see that he'd taken her advice and had a fire blazing.

Elizabeth went to the woman's bedside and saw that the infant was nursing comfortably and the woman's bleeding was normal. She gave her a balm of beeswax, chamomile and tansy to rub on her nipples. Satisfied that her patient was comfortable, she said her goodbyes and accepted the coins and the tin of tea that were held out to her.

Walking down the street, she felt for the coins in her pocket. Bringing out her hand, she saw an assortment of currencies. Some were British and some from the colonies. Luckily, there was one Spanish dollar, the preferred currency. The tea in her sack was especially welcome.

Barter was not unusual. The *habitants* were paying their taxes in chickens these days! The feudal system that was established from the beginning of *Nouvelle-France* was not working well. The families were huge and they didn't earn enough to buy more land. Though they were poor, she preferred to serve those humble, hard-working people. It was not her intention to serve the English as she'd just done, but how could she have refused?

She hoped that in the future, she wouldn't be put in such a conflict between Christian duty and her hatred of the British. That ended her musings and now her thoughts went to putting the kettle on as soon as she got home and to savoring the tea that she so justly deserved.

The loyalists from the American colonies who fled to Canada received a warm welcome from the British while the French *Canadiens* and the Indians were kept in submission since the *Conquest*. The first two governors appointed by the British attempted to achieve a level of fairness, but the British Monarchy preferred to keep the French in their place. To be called French Canadians added to the insult for were they not *Les Canadiens*? Elizabeth resented not only the influences of the British, but also some of the customs that came from France.

From the beginning of the settlement, priests had insisted that midwives take an oath that they would baptize any infant who appeared to be near death. She resented this intrusion. She was also shocked that the wives of officials or wives of wealthy men practiced the French custom of sending their infants off to the countryside to live with wet nurses for two years.

Even her son, Charles, named after his father, had considered doing so after the birth of his first child. He was an entrepreneur and saw it as a sign of high status. Fortunately, she was able to convince her daughter- in-law that it would be a poor choice for her and for the child.

Gradually, the number of Anglo doctors increased and English women preferred to have their babies delivered by these men. Elizabeth had given birth to nine children. Two had died in infancy, but she continued her practice of midwifery, dividing the chores of the household among her two remaining daughters and two sons as she spread her practice farther and farther to serve the *habitants*.

After the boating accident one year before, with the loss of three beloved daughters, she was even more determined to bring life into this world.

On both sides of the family, there were priests, brothers and nuns.

Elizabeth was devout, attending mass every Sunday and on Holy Days unless there was a child to deliver. Why then had she had to pay such a huge price, losing three daughters in that instant when a wind came from nowhere causing their small boat to capsize? They were just out on the river for pleasure and had taken a picnic. They were good sailors and the eldest of the three was fourteen. She had learned to sail from her Papa from the time she was six.

Elizabeth found no answers. Her faith shaken, she prayed less for the souls of her daughters than for her own salvation. She knew they were in heaven. She prayed that God would help her to survive this pain that pierced her heart every breathing moment.

Some years earlier, their son, Jerome, had entered the seminary in Quebec. He seemed to be more interested in studying architecture than religion. Influenced by his paternal uncles, Father Louis and Brother Alexis, who were both Recollets, after completing his studies, he was teaching there.

The Recollets, the first religious order to come to New France had made little progress with the conversion of Indians for they were more suited to a life of the mind. It wasn't until the aggressive Jesuits came that the real missionary work began.

She recalled Jerome's excitement when he realized he had been accepted. "*Maman*, I can't believe that I will be living in the seminary. I am so grateful to my godfather for leaving me funds for my education."

His godfather, a slater, Mr. Jacquet, a childless widower, had left him two hundred pounds.

How clearly she remembered the day that Jerome came to her while she was baking bread after he'd first visited the seminary.

"I can't believe the orchards and the apothecary. The library is filled with Latin books and books of philosophy. In our city why is it that so few people can read when we have such resources? There is a lovely residence for missionaries and the dining hall is exquisite."

She had looked up at him and rubbed her itchy nose with her wrist, powdering it with flour. "Jerome, I haven't heard you speak of God. Are you there for books and gardens? What are your goals when you leave the seminary?"

He came toward her and wiped the flour from her face. In a soft voice he said, "Perhaps, dear *Maman*, I'll never leave the seminary and I'll teach like my uncles. The contemplative life would quite suit me."

Recalling that tender gesture, she missed him all the more. God had taken him, too, by taking him into His service. There were so few left at home. So many things were changing.

Work in the home was divided amongst Elizabeth, her two remaining daughters, and the family's servants. Her daughters took care of the herb garden in summer. Neighboring women shared the chores of carding, spinning and quilting. Her work as a midwife called her away frequently at all hours of the day or night.

Elizabeth received fruits and vegetables in payment as well as sides of pork and venison.

As a midwife, she did far more than deliver babies. She was called upon when there was illness in the families, for she had many formulas for relieving sore throat, rashes, headache, and fever. She also made poultices for pain. She was there too when life ended. She sewed stillborn babies into their shrouds and sadly, she had once wrapped a dead child and placed it in the arms of his mother who had also expired. The child had been born two days earlier and suddenly she was called to the home where they both lay dying. Little did she know that the rosy rash on both mother and child was a symptom of scarlet fever, a far more serious disease that could spread to other family members with no other visible sign.

Her husband, Charles, was often away tending to his lumber business. The trees in this part of Canada grew straight up to the sky and the varieties of hardwood were very much in demand in France. But now, the new government forbade all import and export business with the Mother Country. Charles had to find other sources to buy his logs.

At home, though he and Elizabeth shared their bed, theirs was more of a partnership. Each had a set of responsibilities and, as long as all went well, they gave little thought to the other. This had changed for a while with the loss of their three daughters. Night after night, they had clung to each other in wordless sorrow. But now, there was even more distance between them. Charles was happy for Jerome's occasional visits, though his youngest son was nothing like him, for he had no interest in land acquisition or business. He respected the young man's brilliant mind and sometimes discussed business problems with him.

The pressing problem was the export of his lumber, but no conversation with Jerome could stay away from books for very long.

After hearing of his father's predicament, Jerome quickly retorted, "Perhaps the people of France have more respect for us now that they can't buy our lumber and our iron ore, and they realize how much they benefited from our resources. That foolish man, *Monsieur Buffon*, discredited our land so much in his books!"

"Who is this Monsieur Buffon and what does his opinion have to do with my lumber business?" Charles asked, immediately aware that he was being sidetracked.

"He wrote that everything here is inferior in *Nouvelle-France*, and even said that our animals were smaller than those of Europe. He almost went as far as to call the Indians imbeciles. I think he got his information from amateurs who visited for a short time and never set foot in our forests. We have all of his books at the seminary. Why we keep them, I don't know, for it's thirty-six volumes of misinformation!"

Elizabeth, who was preparing their evening meal, overheard the conversation and said, "If he ever thought our animals were smaller, he should have been with me the other day at the home of one of the *habitants* when a moose came right up to the cabin. It was the biggest beast I have ever seen and such antlers!"

"*Maman*, the biggest are six or seven feet tall at the shoulder and weigh up to fifteen hundred pounds. They are second only to the whale when it comes to mammals!"

Jerome, with his encyclopedic knowledge annoyed his father who quickly came back to the problem at hand.

"Elizabeth, I am speaking to our son. No more diversion please. I don't care what anyone thinks about the size of our animals, I just have to find a market for my lumber."

Realizing that information from books was not of any interest to his father, the young man turned his attention to his concerns.

"I'm sure the people of the American colonies have some need for lumber, Papa. Why don't you try to find buyers along Lake Champlain?"

The suggestion proved to be a valid one, for the boundaries between Quebec and the colonies were not so clearly defined.

In time, Charles Demers managed to do some commerce with the colonists. In addition, there was a market for lumber with all the new arrivals from Europe. The family would not starve after all.

CHAPTER 7
THE *HABITANTS*

I n rural areas, the people made no progress under the *habitant* system, a remnant of the European feudal era. Almost all of the great landowners had returned to France, and the small farms could no longer support the families that numbered sixteen children or more. Surrounded by new arrivals that included the Irish, Germans, and the Whigs, this over-population resulted in a shortage of land and no room for expansion. Besides, there was no banking system to make it possible to acquire small loans with which to buy land.

In the towns, the children had opportunities for learning at the convents, but outside of Quebec City or Montreal, education was very limited. Children were needed for their labor. Farmers couldn't earn enough for their produce; the roads were bad; the growing season short and crop rotation unheard of. The *habitants* still had to pay tithes to the church. Everyone worked from sunrise to sunset. There was no time for childhood. Infant mortality rose because of increasing poverty.

Elizabeth was called out into the countryside to deliver babies several times a week. The first frost came in October. She would use snowshoes to reach the small farms, or she would go on horseback, fording half-frozen streams with strong currents. She could go by boat until the rivers froze. The citizens who lived near the streams and rivers were ordered to provide and maintain ropes, canoes and small boats for crossings. The streams, lakes, and rivers were many.

If it wasn't snow she encountered it was pounding rain or hail. Her babies didn't wait for sunshine and blue skies. In fact, they seemed to prefer full moon nights.

The roads to the small farms away from the St. Lawrence River were often mere paths and maintenance of them was the responsibility of the people who lived nearby.

Sometimes a family member came out to meet her carrying a lantern to guide her where a young woman was in labor. Darkness came early in autumn. She had to leave her clothes outside upon returning home for she often picked up lice from the unsanitary conditions in the crowded homes.

"Do your children attend school?" she would ask. More often than not, the answer was "No. There's no time for school. We need the children here on our small farms or we won't have enough to eat come winter." Books were nowhere in sight.

Early one morning, a woman came to her door. Elizabeth recognized her as the neighbor of a woman who had died in childbirth less than a year before. The woman, Mrs. Paquette, led her to the same humble cottage where the death had occurred.

"But who is with child in this home?" she asked. A ten-month-old infant lay in a cradle nearby. The neighbor who had come for her responded, "The eldest daughter who is just fourteen." It wasn't the first time that Elizabeth had heard of such a thing.

Two other neighbors were inside tending to the young woman. They gave knowing glances in order to spare her feelings.

"Poor young thing, she probably doesn't even know how she got in a family way," whispered one woman.

On the bed, gnashing her teeth and desperately trying to push the baby out, the girl was making inhuman sounds and tugging desperately at the sheets tied to the head rail. Two women held her legs apart.

Elizabeth had arrived just in time. The baby had to be turned. Though the birth was difficult, both survived. The neighbors prepared food for everyone and stayed with the new mother.

As Elizabeth washed up at the basin, one neighbor rested on the floor before the fire, for she'd been there through the night. It had been a long, painful labor. The girl's father was nowhere in sight.

The worst times came for Elizabeth when after all her efforts, she'd have to call for the surgeon whose sad job was to remove the fetus with his surgical tools.

Sometimes it was possible to save one life or the other, but often not. She would stay to help sew the burial garments for both mother and infant.

Relieved that this young girl would survive, but very much afraid for the girl's future, she resolved to speak to the parish priest. After stopping at the parish house, Elizabeth returned home, thankful for the exhaustion that took over her body and mind, and hopeful for a night of blissful sleep.

But after a few hours, she would awaken and relive those last days in her kitchen when her daughters were packing their picnic.

The population of Canada was growing. The increase in numbers came from Irish, English, Germans and Scots who were comfortable living under the British flag.

The French, surrounded by people who did not speak their language, nor would they ever speak theirs, were joined by yet another group of outsiders, one of French speakers. They joined the *habitants* and they were poorer and unwelcome by the struggling Quebecois. These were the Acadians who'd been driven from their fertile lands.

From 1765 to 1763 these poor souls who'd owned and tilled their farms in Acadia for several generations had been pawns of the French and victims of the British who planned to force back the French boundaries from all quarters. Several thousand of them had removed to Cape Breton where, dominated by the French missionary *Le Loutre* , they were threatened with hell if they didn't support King Louie. They were told that fidelity to the King was equal to fidelity to God. An even worse threat was that he, *Le Loutre*, would set his army of savages upon them, and the result would be unbearable torture and then death. His Indian followers were eager to set upon their victims for they could become rich on scalp wages. *La Loutre* received a large budget from the King for payment of scalps.

After the French ceded the land to British control, the Acadians were forbidden to cooperate with that government. Because of the lack of cooperation, the British determined to purge Acadia of every French inhabitant. Only a small number made their way to Quebec.

Elizabeth entered the wretched home of a *habitant* family who had given refuge to a young Acadian woman. She'd been in labor for sixteen hours. Under her ministrations, the birth went well.

Matilde, the young woman, was a survivor of the final endeavor by the British to remove every original settler from *Beausejour*, the largest French settlement on the north side of the Bay of Fundy in Acadia from which the British expected an attack.

Matilde had witnessed the whole terrible ordeal.

CHAPTER 8
THE ORDERS -
NOVA SCOTIA

The Orders

Whereas his Excellency the gGovernor has instructed us of his last resolution respecting the matters proposed lately to the inhabitants and has ordered us to communicate the same to the inhabitants in general in person, His excellency being desirous that each of them should be fully satisfied of His Majesty's intentions, which he has also ordered us to communicate to you, such as they have been given him. We therefore order and strictly enjoin by these presents to all inhabitants as well of the above-named districts as of all the other districts, both old men and young men as well as all the lads of ten years of age, to attend at the church in Grand Pre on Friday, the fifth instant at three of the clock in the afternoon, that we may impart what we are ordered to communicate to them; declaring that no excuse will be admitted on any pretense whatsoever, on pain of forfeiting goods and chattels in default..

Given at Grand Pre the second of September, in the twenty-ninth year of his Majesty's reign, A.D. 1755

By this order you are called to hear his Majesty's final resolution. For half a century the Governor of Nova Scotia has granted you more indulgences than any other subjects but you have refused alliance. You will forfeit your land, your cattle and livestock and be removed from this provence.

Matilde spoke. "Our crops were ready for harvest. We had all worked so hard to see this day under the clear skies. How could we know what awaited us until the men were forced to attend that meeting in the church?"

Just twenty years old and pregnant, she had hidden in a haystack on that fateful day when the King's soldiers and two thousand volunteers from New England, among them fishermen, farmers, shopkeepers who'd mustered in Boston and been given clothes and blankets, sailed to join British troops in *Beausejour*. The New Englanders had enlisted for one year. There'd been skirmishes with the French at the Fort.

When the Acadians refused to take an oath of loyalty, and had shown signs of hostility, the British, realizing that the New England troops were nearing the end of their period of enlistment, put the plan to remove the French into action.

By early November, 1,510 persons were sent off in eleven vessels. By the end of the month, 1,664 had been sent from Annapolis.

Governor Winslow was charged with the execution of this plan. He tried to keep families together but wasn't always successful. He urged his soldiers to carry out the orders with care 'that an end may be put to distressing this distressed people.'

Matilde recounted her story to Elizabeth after the delivery of her child, a boy. "When the last ships departed I hid in a haystack. I had nothing but cheese for three days. I saw the beautiful farms burning. The cows were making horrible sounds, for they hadn't been milked. The animals in the coops ran out of food. Many were burned in the barns and pens after the troops had gathered what they wanted and what they could manage to take away. The stench of burning flesh was horrible. I saw hell. I knew I would never see my husband, my brothers or my father again. I just ran through the woods until I met some savages who helped me. They gave me food and water and tended to my cuts and bruises. They let me stay with their families for a few days, though they were in as much danger as I, were they to be caught. I had cousins in Quebec and made my way here. It was weeks before I found my relatives."

Her cousin Jeanette added, "When Matilde finally found us, she was exhausted and hysterical. She was covered with scratches and bruises, and her hair was matted. She couldn't speak. It took several weeks for her to recover. It's a miracle that she didn't lose the baby."

Matilde began to speak again. "When the men went to the church, they were told to return the next day with just one bag. Many ships were in the harbor. The men were deemed prisoners. All were in shock. The next day, they were lined up. The women screamed and children wept.

While the ships waited to sail away, some women rowed out with provisions for them. Some threw themselves on the ships. After they set sail, orders were given to burn all the farms and farmhouses. Two men who tried to escape were shot. This went on for days. Some people carried the elderly in wheelbarrows. My husband, Claude, told me to stay away. He feared for my safety. He left money for me in a small pouch before lining up with the others. I'll never forget his strong arms around me before he walked out the door."

Looking at the young mother with the baby in her arms, Elizabeth thought that Matilde was lucky indeed to have found relatives who would share what little they had, for she'd heard gruesome tales from the Ursuline Sisters about the treatment of other Acadians who'd made their way to Canada.

Some had come from Boston where they'd been dropped off by British ships, but in Quebec their treatment was worse than they'd received from the heretics and they made their way back to New England.

A story that was making the rounds in Quebec was that one unscrupulous Canadian who had many debts took on a number of Acadians to board and lodge. Locking them in his premises, he starved and froze them to death to get the money they had. Poverty left little room for compassion.

CHAPTER 9
BRITISH RULE BEGINS

B ritish General James Murray was appointed first Governor of
Quebec in 1760. A fair man, he was concerned about the rule
that all juries should consist of English only. He strongly disagreed!
"Ten thousand families? We are asking for trouble. There are so few
of us in charge!"

Six years later, he was called back to Britain and General Carlton
was sent in his place, but Carlton was even more worried, for now
France was supporting the American colonies in their rebellion
against England.

He feared that the influence would reach Quebec, as indeed it
had when Thomas Walker, a colonist, invited the Canadians to join
the American rebellion.

On December 8, 1775, two patriot armies led by Benedict
Arnold and General Montgomery were en route to attack Quebec
in hopes of conquering the British.

When the British Governor Carleton got word of this through
his spies, he would not make the mistake made by Montcalm. He
waited for the enemy to come to him.

The first house the patriots reached was *La Potasse*. Thinking it
deserted, they marched past it, but were suddenly attacked by British

soldiers from within.

Right after calling out, "Forward men. Quebec is ours!" Montgomery was killed, and Arnold was wounded. Carleton's spies had known the precise time the attack would occur.

The patriot armies never took control of the city, and later, Benedict Arnold went back to the British side. The political tensions increased after the attempted siege of Quebec by the patriots thirteen years earlier.

Charles Demers, tired of conflict and repression, decided to sell their valuable land holdings in Quebec City and Montreal as he saw the expansion and the increasing population of non-French speaking immigrants.

In 1788, he purchased land northeast of Montreal and divided the properties among his sons, keeping a large parcel for himself.

At supper, with the whole family staring down at their plates and concentrating on eating, he'd exclaim, "We wish to be dominated neither by the British nor the Colonists. We must expand and remove ourselves from both influences." He would become quiet and pensive again, and after a time, he'd repeat his plan to leave. It was not a surprise to his wife and family when the property was sold. They prepared to move.

Elizabeth feared starting over and leaving the city of Quebec, but she had no choice but to follow her husband's will.

"As long as I'm on my beautiful river," she told a neighbor, "I can still get to Montreal, Trois Rivieres and Quebec City." The highway was one hundred and fifty miles from Quebec City to Montreal with Trois Rivieres in between. It would take four and a half days to go from one end to the other, but Charles had purchased land in Lavaltrie and Lanoraie. Neither town was very far from Montreal. Though her trips would be few, she clung to this thought. It would have been difficult for her to live a rural life after her years of living in a city.

Once they were settled in the small villages along the King's Highway facing the river, they heard only their own language, and there was some semblance of their earlier life. But in Quebec City, the British worked to make life better for their people and continued their repression of the French Canadians.

Not all of his countrymen agreed with Charles, who retreated to the countryside with his family. They preferred to stand their ground. At the start of the American Revolution in 1776, there were battalions organized in Quebec to go to the aid of the colonies. When Henry Laurent, a cousin, first heard that Charles was planning to sell his property and land, he said,

"We have a common enemy, the British. Our mother country, France has entered the war. We should help them." He was one man of several who fought under General Washington who was now against the British in the colonies. These men truly believed that living in a democracy was worth fighting for.

When the war ended, Henry Laurent was among those who were not allowed to return to Canada. Their homes and lands were taken over by the British. They were considered traitors by one side and heroes by the U.S. Congress. The state of New York gave them land along the shores of Lake Champlain known as the "Refugees Tract." Each of the 226 soldiers who had served in a regiment known as Congress' Own received from 80 to 240 acres. Among them were Charles' neighbors, Presque Asselin and Albert Trahan.

In the new townships that were formed east of Montreal, the Church was the center of all activity. It was the priest along with the town officials who ordered the citizens to maintain the roads in front of their houses and who supervised the projects.

Nicholas, Charles' favorite and youngest son, was an entrepreneur and had already established a lucrative bakery and a tavern in Lavaltrie. Nicholas also was the most vocal about the inadequate representation of the French, or the true Canadians in the government, and his fervor would not be lost on his future children. Men gathered in the tavern where there were heated discussions about the political situation. Ownership gave Nicholas the opportunity to hold forth at these gatherings.

"Here, I don't need to pass their government offices and be reminded of our lack of power."

His four brothers were trying to eke out a living on their farms and supplemented their meager incomes by selling peat. In his youth, Nicholas had joined them in the summer to work in the bogs. It wasn't long before he decided that it was not the life for him. It was back-breaking work and dangerous. The bogs were deep in some places, as much as fifteen meters. Animals sometimes disappeared in them. The cut peat had to be dried and, when wet, it weighed over a hundred pounds per block. There was a steady market for it as cheap fuel for those families who couldn't afford coal, but the habitants needed much of it to heat their own homes.

The roads were bad, especially the lanes that connected range roads where farmers lived. Getting goods to market was difficult until they reached the mill roads where they had their grain ground into flour. The church forbade any form of limiting the number of children.

The *Monsieur le Cure* was the guardian of his flock or was he another master?

There was one consolation. In these new villages daily life was reminiscent of the days before the conquest, while in Quebec City, the British practiced total domination.

.

CHAPTER *10*
A WEDDING IN LANORAIE
1790

It had been snowing for three days. Nicholas Demers and Rosalie Bonin were to be wed, but the snowstorm that continued on that February day was so fierce that the wedding had to be postponed. Many guests from this small town had been invited. The concern was for those who were coming from Pointe Aux Trembles and Montreal, for they included the parents of Nicholas, Charles and Charlotte Demers.

Rosalie's mother, after seeing the drifting snow, went to her sons' bedroom and grabbed the arm of the nearest boy. "Go to our neighbor Theo's house. He's the only one who can reach the Demers family with his sleigh and his team of dogs. The river is frozen and if he follows it, he won't lose his way. Give him this note to carry. It assures them that the wedding will not be held without them. It will take place next week." The young man, barely awake and rubbing the sleep from his eyes, grudgingly got dressed, and carried out the errand.

An hour later, Theo and his two strong dogs were off for Montreal in the blinding snow.

Nicholas, the prospective groom, had not even considered marriage until he had established himself in Lavaltrie. He had worked tirelessly building his own house, and then establishing a bakery. The tavern came next, for he saw that the town needed a gathering place. It became a regular stopping place for every man in the village after work.

After sending the messenger, Rosalie's mother's mind was elsewhere for she was concerned about all the food that had been prepared.

"The poor will eat well today. I'm going to the convent to distribute some of this food. We'll take the pork pies and the mincemeat cookies. Those pheasants should go too. We'll have to cook all week to prepare another wedding dinner. When will this snow end?"

When she looked over at Rosalie, the young woman had tears in her eyes.

"I know what a disappointment this is to you, but our only choice would have been to have the wedding without Nicholas' family, and that wouldn't have been proper. We'll wait it out. It's God's will."

Their home was near the church and the convent where the good sisters took in indigents and orphans who would enjoy the food even more than the wedding guests.

"The cakes will keep so at least we needn't bake more! The ingredients of rum and dried fruit were so expensive. She added more rum to a cloth and placed it over the small cakes that were arranged in a circle and three layers. "This will keep them moist. Tonight we'll dine on Easter pie, for it won't keep, but we'll invite our neighbors in and no one will mind repeating it on the actual day of the wedding!"

Indeed they wouldn't for it was a succulent dish that included wild turkey, chicken, rabbit, partridges, and pigeons flavored with delicious spices and onions. It was baked in a high crust in the oven at the bakery.

After preparing baskets and wrapping food, Rosalie and her mother dressed in their warmest clothes and made several trips to the convent trudging through the snow. Their snowshoes hardly helped for they sank in the wet snow. They were met at the door by beaming faces. Hands reached out eagerly to receive the baskets.

Even though they stood there for a short time, Rosalie and her mother couldn't help noticing the bleak interior and the plain clothes worn by the children who came to the door. There was even a musty smell that came from inside. Only the sister seemed fresh in her black and white habit.

Back in their home, the Easter pie was placed on the table where it made a grand centerpiece. The delicious aroma wafted throughout the house and even the family dog *Petite Blanche* walked around the table with her nose held high sniffing the air.

Nicholas wasn't invited to dine with them that afternoon, for the menu had to be a surprise for him and his parents on the day of the wedding.

The grand event took place a week later and sunshine filled the small church. The four feet of snow that had fallen was hard packed and the guests had arrived in sleighs.

After a long nuptial mass, the guests returned to the home of Rosalie's parents and were welcomed by a wonderful feast. The priest said a prayer before the meal, his face red from the effects of several glasses of wine.

Nicholas glanced at Rosalie who was ten years younger than he, overcome by her beauty and her strong mind, he felt at that moment that he'd accomplished all of his goals. They would have a secure future together.

He thought of the night ahead when the guests would leave and he felt his blood surge. At that moment, Rosalie caught his eye and lowered her head. Had she read his mind?

Fine wines and brandies accompanied the meal and there was music and dancing.

For his *habitant* brothers, this window into a life of prosperity would only fuel their resentment of their own lives on their meager farms.

"But why persevere if you are getting nowhere?" Nicholas said as he stood with his brother, George, who had been drinking heavily. George was lamenting his failure as a provider for his large family.

Nicholas advised, "There are opportunities in lumber. You and your sons can work part-time in the lumber business. Why not open your own sawmill? There's a great need for lumber right here in Lavaltrie."

George drained his glass of brandy and said angrily, "I already owe money to those damnable peddlers who come door-to-door selling farm equipment. The last thing I bought was a peat press, some contraption that was supposed to make blocks from bits of peat and to keep it from being wasted. All that it wasted was my money! One bad crop and I got behind in my payments. I'll never catch up. I wake up every morning to a complaining wife and hungry children and growing debts."

Nicholas refilled George's glass. There would be no fine brandy or wine in his humble home.

One or more of their children might escape a life of ignorance by going into the clergy, but most of them would know nothing of the world beyond, and their small world held no hope for the future. The families were held together by the faith and perseverance of the women who here in Canada had more authority than they'd ever had in France. During these difficult years, it was *Maman* and the parish priests who guided their flocks.

CHAPTER 11

THE PAPINEAU
REBELLION - 1837

Nicholas and Rosalie Demers would have fourteen children. The bakery expanded to provide work for six of their sons. The eldest, who had returned to Quebec City, was one of the followers of Joseph Papineau in the rebellion of 1837.

Mr. Papineau, a native of Montreal, was a lawyer of the land-owning seigniorial class who entered politics. He was a brilliant orator. In 1834, together with his colleagues he drafted a document of 92 resolutions that called for an American style democracy. The answer to their requests came three years later. Only ten of the resolutions were accepted.

In the meantime, the government became even more oppressive. Papineau's answer was to suggest that the people boycott British goods and that they form an alternative government. In general, he favored non-violence but the farmers became more and more agitated after a season when disease had destroyed most of their crops. There were also urban rebels who felt it was time for more extreme measures.

When two young men, Joseph Cardinal and Joseph Duquet raided an Indian village to procure arms, they were arrested and sentenced to death. The very people that they stole from pleaded for their lives.

Following are the words of the Saut Saint-Louis tribal members:

'That we felt a profound pain upon learning that our Father had resolved to put to death two of the prisoners we took, Joseph N. Cardinal and Joseph Duquet. We come then to our father to ask him to save the lives of these unfortunate men. They did us no harm. They didn't dip their hands in the blood of their brothers. Why spread theirs? If there must be victims, there are others besides these unhappy ones who are more guilty than they.

The wife and children of one, the elderly mother of the other, join their tears to our voices to beg for your mercy.

The services we've rendered to His Majesty, those that he yet expects of us and that we won't hesitate to render him when the occasion presents, leads us to believe that our humble prayer will find the path to the heart of your Excellency.'

Canada's Governor-General read the petition. Both men were executed. Bloody confrontations followed.

A warrant went out for Papineau's arrest, accusing him of high treason. With Dr. Nelson, an Anglo supporter, and Dr. Cote they announced to the crowds that it was time for armed insurrection. At the height of the rebellion, two thousand rebels armed with clubs and pitchforks rioted in several villages.

A young habitant woman reported seeing thousands of British soldiers newly arrived from England, marching along the King's Highway. Among them were the Royal Scots, the Glengarry Highlanders. They were called out to end the insurrection and end it they did, with a six- mile swath of devastation. Churches and farms were burned; crops destroyed leaving families to starve. Hundreds were arrested and twelve were hanged in Lower Canada.

Some of the patriots fled to the United States, including Papineau, who some accused of cowardice for leaving. In Vermont there was already a small French Canadian settlement. There, Duvernay, one of the leaders of the rebellion, published the first French newspaper, *Le Patriote*. Of those who remained in Canada, many were imprisoned. Others were deported to Australia and Bermuda.

In 1841 Upper and Lower Canada were united. The British government decreed that from now on there would be one official language, English.

The short-lived attempts at revolution were over. Now, the important thing became *La Survivance*, the survival of a culture.

CHAPTER 12
LA SURVIVANCE- THE SURVIVAL OF A CULTURE

B etween 1855 and 1890, eight million immigrants flowed into New York City through Ellis Island. Earlier, from Canada, between 1840 and 1930 over 900,000 Quebecois traveled to the United States, and primarily to Maine, New Hampshire, Vermont, Massachusetts, Connecticut and Rhode Island.

The latter group would go largely unnoticed in the United States except in New England, for the Quebecois often returned to their towns and villages in Quebec, over a rather loose border. Eventually, they stayed, for life in Canada had become too difficult.

During the potato famine in Ireland, over half a million Irish were evicted from their cottages. These starving people were put on ships with their passage paid for by their landlords. The first of these ships were bound for Quebec. The journey took from six weeks to three months. Many of the passengers were infected with typhus. So many died on the ships that they came to be known as Coffin Ships. A fifteen-day quarantine period meant that many healthy Irish died after staying in the lice-infested holds. Hundreds of bodies were dumped into the Saint Laurence River where waiting ships lined up with their human cargo.

The Sisters who tried to nurse the sick who arrived in Quebec often succumbed to disease or died of exhaustion. There were only one hundred and fifty beds in their small hospital and the lines of sick and dying were endless.

The surviving Irish, jobless and homeless, wandered the streets of Montreal and Quebec contributing to the already strained economic conditions.

In Canada, in 1846, the British repealed protective tariffs that prevented the Americans from unlimited selling of their products on Canada's markets. The Canadian farmers with their three-month growing season and outmoded farming methods couldn't compete. Milling and lumber industries suffered as well. City dwellers also found it hard to find jobs. They were the first to cross the border whether on foot, by lumber wagon, or later by rail.

The disheartened farmers were to follow, attracted by American industrialization in New England and the never-ending need for workers in the textile mills.

Watching their friends and neighbors make the journey was painful for the family of Francois Demers and his wife, Leonore, who had married in Lanoraie, those many years ago. Their small family businesses were sufficient to keep them from considering such a move, but tragedy struck the next generation when their second son, Eusebe Demers, and Theotiste, his wife, the parents of twelve children, died of influenza in 1880 within days of each other.

Their eldest daughter, Antoinette was in a nunnery in Quebec City and about to take her final vows. The next in line was Jean-Baptiste, just seventeen years old. Then came Edouard and Alexis, a few years younger.

After the funeral, the older children realized their plight. They had eight younger brothers and sisters under the age of fourteen.

There was no one to care for them, at least not permanently. They found that their father's business, a small dry goods store, was almost bankrupt. Customers were steady, and it wasn't until they discovered the credit slips in their father's receipt book that the sons realized that it would be impossible to collect all of these debts. Their neighbors were in even more precarious straits. The family still owned some land west of Montreal, but they weren't farmers nor were they lumbermen.

Jean-Baptiste soon took over the role as head of family. The eldest, he was the most serious and pensive. He had an uncanny sense of mathematics and had been a promising pupil. The parish priest had tried to encourage him to join the clergy, but it was the last thing on his mind. "Even before the death of our parents, I've dreamed of going to Massachusetts. There is no attraction for me in Maine. I don't want to work in their sweatshops. The Gervais have come back from Southbridge several times. I've met with them and I like what I hear. The town is prosperous and has a large Canadian community. The Langevins have business there, too. I've decided to go."

Alexis was astonished. "You mean that you've thought of this all along? Why is it that you never spoke of it?"

"I never mentioned it in front of Papa, for he would never have considered leaving here, but on his last visit, Mr. Gervais offered me a job in his grocery store in Southbridge. The town is thriving, and he needs more help. If you all want to follow, I think it's our only solution with the little ones. We'll find work for the four of us and we'll find someone to take care of the younger ones." Clutching his leg, little Marion who was just four, began to weep, "Don't go. I want *maman*. Make Antoinette come back." Jean Baptiste picked her up and smoothed her dark curls. He wiped her tears with his handkerchief. "Blow your nose, and be a big girl, Marion. Just think, when I come back for you, you'll get to ride on a train and have adventures. Wouldn't you like that?" By now, train travel was efficient and went as far as Massachusetts.

He turned to his brothers, "After the funeral, I thought of trying to convince Antoinette that the family needed her more than the church, but she wouldn't leave the convent." As he spoke, Marion snuggled against his shoulder and closed her eyes, but she gripped him tightly. Unfastening her arms, Jean Baptiste said, "Don't worry. We won't be leaving right away. Go outside with your brothers. They're watching Father Crow. Maybe they're playing the hide and seek game with him."

Four years earlier, their mother, Theotiste, had found the injured crow beneath the kitchen window, and nursed it back to health. A fledgling, she had encouraged it to fly away, but it rarely left her side. She often walked around the house with it on her shoulder, and whenever she went outside, Father Crow would stand on her head. The crow sat on her coffin for days during the wake.

Outside, Marion found three of her brothers. The children were playing their usual game with the bird. They enjoyed placing bits of corn under a cloth. The bird would pull the cloth away with its beak and find the corn.

They often played variations of this game with Father Crow, sometimes hiding a small toy, or a shiny object. He persevered until the object was found. Their laughter reached the brothers inside the house, who continued their serious discussion.

"Maybe Edouard and I will go first. We'll settle our debts here and take whatever is left to start a new life." Jean-Baptiste turned to Alexis. "I'll need you to settle things here."

The Church was the heart of the community and the Quebecois Mother was the heart and the center of the family, but dear *Maman* was dead. Their family was without a center and these young people would be tossed into an uncertain future. However, they would find that they had a strong pilot at their helm.

THE SECOND MIGRATION
PART 3

CHAPTER 1
SOUTHBRIDGE, MASSACHUSETTS

The government of the Province of Quebec, worried about the huge numbers of people who were leaving, published horror stories about the circumstances they would encounter upon their arrival in New England.

These stories couldn't have been farther from the truth. For many who had come from rural areas, their arrival there meant that they'd have running water and electricity for the first time in their lives as well as a living wage. For those of an entrepreneurial nature, even with minimal education, the move meant opportunity.

One common story that came from the government and the priest in the pulpit was to report that the émigrés didn't return home because they were too poor to afford the fare by train or any other means of transportation.

In spite of this propaganda, neighbors followed neighbors, and relatives followed relatives. Whole villages removed to the same towns in New England.

Fall River, Massachusetts was one of the most popular destinations because of its cotton mills. By 1875 the mills were producing over 340 million yards of cotton.

Woolen mills, print shops, and iron works, all mechanical wonders, soon followed.

Given the increased number of establishments, the loss of American workers resulting from the westward movement, and the loss of manpower after the Civil War, new workers were welcomed and needed. The industrial revolution in New England was moving full speed ahead!

Manufacturing was growing in Quebec as well, but at a much slower pace, partly because of the archaic banking system. Wages were much lower than those paid across the border.

The Catholic Church, too, was losing its flock. After hearing that the Demers family was planning to leave Lanoraie, Monsieur Le Cure went to their home. He was determined to discourage them from carrying out their plans. After a few futile arguments, he was quickly interrupted. "My God," said Jean Baptiste, "if you think for a moment that I would give up this country and this culture for some frivolous reason you are sadly mistaken! You know me well enough to know otherwise. Poverty is at our door and debts will suffocate our whole family. Exile which lies just hours away is a better choice for my brothers and sisters than a life here of pain and privation."

Monsieur Le Cure cut his visit short. It wasn't the first time he'd heard such responses to his pleas.

Realizing that it would be the only way to keep its parishioners, the church hierarchy in Canada gradually assigned priests to establish parishes wherever French communities sprang up in New England. The priests accepted these assignments with some eagerness, perhaps out of religious zeal, but perhaps they too were attracted by better living conditions and salaries after hearing from those who'd gone before them.

Just days after the Curate's visit, Jean Baptiste had an opportunity to speak with his former neighbor, Mr. Gervais. He had returned to Canada to escort more family members and other potential workers to Southbridge, Massachusetts.

He had been in Southbridge for less than a year and now his company had sent him back to recruit workers. He spent the first few days driving through rural areas with a team of horses pulling a large wagon that held as many as sixteen passengers. He carried advertisements for spinners and weavers. There was also a need for fine needlework to mend errors in the woolens that were ready for shipment. This was one of the highest paying jobs. Advertisements had been posted in the small villages some weeks before. Young women jumped right onboard with one suitcase when they heard the wagon was in town, knowing they'd have free passage to Massachusetts and a place to live.

Jean Baptiste joined him at a table in a nearby tavern with other neighbors, and after serving Gervais a drink, he encouraged his friend to tell the group about his experiences.

Gervais was enthusiastic and soon gained the group's attention.

"We took a boat to Montreal and went directly to the *Gare Bonaventure*. There, my family waited while I bought tickets from an agency on Rue St. Jacques. The agent was helpful in every way, explaining the trip down to the minutest detail.

We traveled on the Passumpsic Railroad after the agent informed me that not only was it the cheapest but it had the most extensive routes in Canada and New England. After my travel expenses were paid, I had thirty dollars to my name." He paused just long enough to take a drink.

"We traveled all night in comfortable cars and after going through Vermont and New Hampshire, we arrived in Lowell, Massachusetts, a distance of a little over three hundred miles. The cost of that ticket was just ten dollars. You won't believe that train station! It is an architectural wonder. It has newspaper stands, restaurants, a telegraph office, separate waiting rooms for men and women, even a tobacco shop. You'll have to see it for yourselves!" As soon as he had a chance to interrupt, Jean Baptiste voiced one major concern. "How did you manage since you speak no English?"

"I was pleased to find that all the agents were bilingual. They could speak English and French as well as write in both languages. Formerly, there'd been abuses on the other railroad lines especially since people from Quebec were traveling by the cheapest fare, and the railroad employees couldn't understand them. But this railroad company changed all that. You won't lack for anything on these trains."

"How long was the trip?" Jean Baptiste asked.

"Less than twenty- four hours after leaving Montreal, after a short wait in Lowell and another hour on a train, we were in Southbridge. There, we had jobs, a comfortable place to live, vouchers for food for the first week, and my family didn't have to start working until the following Monday."

Jean Baptiste and the others continued with their questioning for several hours, but one thing that Mr. Gervais failed to mention was that their first night under a strange roof, exhausted from their journey and realizing that they were now immigrants, each family member, just moments before sleep, experienced that melancholy that we call homesickness.

CHAPTER 2
LEAVING LAVALTRIE: THE PLAN

N o sooner had Mr. Gervais left, than Jean Baptiste started to put his own plan into action, relating all the information to his brothers.

Less than four months later, he and Edouard arrived in Southbridge with Joe and Louis. The year was 1880. Alexis stayed behind with the younger children. With the exception of Marion, they were in their original house, but little Marion was on a large farm with a cousin who agreed to care for her.

Once in Massachusetts, having reached their destination, the young men were greeted by a town bursting with energy. The population of the town was sixty percent French. Storefront signs bore the names that they'd been familiar with in Quebec, LANGEVIN, GERVAIS LAMOUREUX, MATHIEU LAVALLEE, BOMBARDIER...

Most of the grocery stores and butcher shops were French-owned and all of the businesses had French employees.

Felix Gatineau had a large store where windows were lighted with gaslights and one could buy groceries, hay, grain, meats, and even travel tickets to Canada and the West.

There was one store that stood out for it was larger than all the others on Main Street, and that was the Jacob Edwards Department Store. It was built in 1844 and was the first store of its kind in the United States. The Town Hall was another stunning building that housed a high school on the second floor. The new YMCA dominated the corner of Main and Elm.

As they walked from the railroad station, the brothers were so busy looking around them that they had to be cautioned while crossing the street for there were bicyclists, horse drawn ice wagons, fruit vendors, milk wagons as well as private carriages going down the busy street.

The mill and factory owners saw the wisdom in having middle managers that spoke French. Good communication increased efficiency and gave the newcomers room for advancement. Notre Dame and Sacred Heart, two French-speaking parishes had already been established. The textile mills and the tool and dye company had a large presence.

In Southbridge, in 1833, William Beecher, a jeweler, started making eyeglass frames as part of his business. He created steel-framed spectacles that outranked all others in demand for they were cheaper. He employed four persons.

Beecher retired in 1862 and after going through several owners, the company held a total stock of four hundred shares, forty of which were owned by George Wells who became its president.

It was renamed the American Optical Company in 1869, and was commonly referred to as the AO. It continued to grow and became the major employer from that time on, in the town of twenty-five thousand.

The company's defined goal was 'to manufacture and sell spectacles of gold, silver, steel, and plated metals, also rings and thimbles, and such other like articles as said company may from time to time desire to make.'

As its spectacles became known for their quality and competitive prices, the AO was responsible for an unofficial name for Southbridge,

"The Eyes of the Commonwealth."

The first Catholic Church to be founded was St. Mary's, founded by the Irish. But the French were eager to hear sermons in their own language and wished to establish schools.

Language wasn't the only reason. The Irish were in control of the diocese based in Worcester. There was an Irish bishop and most of the proceeds of their church went to the diocese. The French were accustomed to keeping funds in their own parishes. Their refusal to send church funds to the diocese resulted in the threat of excommunication and it took intervention from the Pope himself to convince the cardinal to appoint a French bishop.

The Demers brothers started their days in the grocery business and it wasn't long before Jean Baptiste and a small group of businessmen founded the Southbridge Savings Bank. Edouard started a small bakery and invested in parcels of land.

Alexis, writing from Canada, announced that he had a sweetheart and planned to marry her as soon as he could bring her to Southbridge. Like him, she was an orphan. He'd been settling matters in Lavaltrie for five years. While his brothers were becoming established in Southbridge, he was barely keeping the rest of the family together. In summer, they had supplemented their income by working on farms, especially at haying time and later for harvests, but this couldn't support them. They were all grateful for the money that they received from their older brothers in Massachusetts, and were eager to join them there.

Alexis and his bride-to-be soon came to Massachusetts with all the children except Marion, who was dearly loved by the farm family that took her in.

Soon after their arrival in Southbridge, banns were announced in the church, followed by a small wedding. Alexis and his bride, Joanna, settled in one of the mill houses owned by Edouard. She was soon pregnant. He had a job at a lumber company. He worked hard in the sawmill loading lumber and delivering it.

The young couple's days together were blissful. At the end of each day of hard work when he knew that he'd see her smiling face, his fatigue melted away, but that joy was short-lived. In her eighth month of pregnancy she went into labor. A doctor was called and after many hours his face told all as he emerged from the bedroom. The baby, a son, was healthy and strong.

"I couldn't save Joanna," he said sorrowfully. I did everything I could, but the bleeding was too much. I put the child in her arms and she was soon gone."

Joanna's aunt and uncle, whose children were grown up, welcomed the new baby to their small white house on Clark Street where little Eugene was taken right after his christening.

After four years, little Eugene's aunt and uncle announced to Alexis that they could no longer take care of the child. Reluctantly, Alexis took him by train and placed him in an orphanage in Quebec, the very orphanage where his sister, Sister Antoinette was the director.

He would see very little of his father, Alexis, for years to come.

CHAPTER 3
ELIZABETH LANGEVIN

E lizabeth Langevin was the eldest of another large Canadian family. She was born in West Warren, Massachusetts in 1872, a first generation American. Her parents had arrived from Canada in the early days of the Quebecois migration, and had struggled far more than the Demers family before getting a foothold in society.

Now, in her mid- twenties, she was a beauty and a popular one. The Langevins, her close relatives, had a prosperous hat shop on Main St. in Southbridge. She was happy to model their creations every Sunday in church. It was a far cry from her early days where, starting at the age of eight, she worked in the cotton mill where she had to stand on a stool to reach the looms.

At that time, the family salary was paid to her papa in one pay envelope. Later, when she received her own envelope at the age of fourteen, she knew she'd have to hand it to her father.

But very cleverly, she managed to change the sum on the envelope to keep just a little for new hair ribbons and an occasional peppermint stick.

The family had moved to Southbridge, and Elizabeth was in love. She had learned English quickly and in her days at Ames Worsted, she caught the eye of a foreman, John Marshall. Now, she was a sales clerk at the hat shop. Ten years her senior, he was not French and he was not Catholic. This information was kept from her parents by having another casual beau, one of whom they'd approve. He would be seen walking her back from the mill from time to time.

She had another secret. She carried the diamond ring from John Marshall around her neck and kept it discreetly tucked inside her high-necked pleated shirtwaist, for he had asked her to marry him.

John boarded in a lovely, small white house on Main Street. The front door off the porch led to a hall and his rooms were directly to the right, so it was easy for her to join him in his sitting room on occasion.

She would slip in on her lunch hour or other pre-arranged times. Otherwise, their meetings were in the park or at dances that she'd attend with her other beau who was sworn to secrecy.

She kept her relationship with Mr. Marshall proper, only allowing a few kisses. On the few occasions when they were alone, they held hands and talked about their future, especially about breaking the news to her family.

He was a tall, handsome man with light skin and green eyes, and a daily customer at Girard's Barber Shop for a shave and a haircut. His clothes were elegantly tailored. Elizabeth noticed that he was unable to resist the long mirror in his entrance hall.

One day, he led Elizabeth to it, and pressing his head close to hers said,

"Mirror mirror on the wall, who is fairest of them all?"

She quickly replied, "You, you snowball!" and pulled away from him.

Elizabeth knew what he was trying to say. He had commented ever so subtly before about her olive complexion and asked if there were *coureurs du bois* in her family who might have something to do with her coloring. The subject did not come up again.

Soon after their agreement to marry, he surprised her with an announcement.

"Gold has been discovered in the Klondike, and I'm going."

Four days after the discovery of gold, every paper had spread the news. It was July of 1897, a time of recession and unemployment in much of the country. Bank failures contributed to the panic. It was also an opportunity for adventurers, for all of the United States had been settled and the Klondike presented a new frontier.

Within days of the news, gold fever spread and forty thousand people from all over the world would descend on the Klondike region in Northwest Canada, just east of the Alaska border. By the next year, so many had gone that there was actually a fear of famine.

John did not intend to leave Elizabeth behind. He insisted that she come along with him.

"You'll wait for me at the Cadillac Hotel in Seattle." He saw a shadow of doubt cross her face.

"Elizabeth, there are doctors, lawyers, businessmen, people from all walks of life heading there. It's a chance of a lifetime. If anyone can make it, I can. I'll do it for us."

Elizabeth was shocked. Could she leave all she knew, family and friends to take such a risk?

"I can't answer now. There are too many things for me to think about." She shook her head from side to side. "I never expected to have to make such a decision." Surprised by her silence, he said, "I'm leaving in three days. I'll be at the train station at 6:00 in the morning on Thursday. Bring one valise. We'll reach Seattle together by the land route."

He didn't tell Elizabeth how difficult this adventure would be. After leaving Seattle, he'd have to hike about forty miles to the headwaters of the Yukon River and then go by raft or boat five hundred miles to Dawson City near the gold fields. Customs and duties imposed by the Northwest Mounted Police would take every cent he had after providing for Elizabeth in Washington.

Little did he know how crowded and rowdy Seattle had become in a few months. Yes, it was one place where the prospectors could get their provisions, but they would also need places to stay while they were preparing for the journey. It wasn't a matter of a pick and shovel. The Canadian government demanded that they have one year's supply of food. They were going to a hostile environment. On one trail alone, three thousand horses died in less than three months. Because it was so treacherous and because of the stench of carrion, Dead Horse Trail had to be closed. Some prospectors came back with gold; some with nothing; and some never came back at all.

Elizabeth would think long and hard. She remembered how happy she felt in his presence, and she remembered his vanity. When the Thursday of his departure came, Elizabeth stood at her bedroom window and wept as she dressed for her usual day at the hat shop. She never heard from John Marshall again, but she wore his ring until the day she died.

In 1910 this notice appeared in the Southbridge News:
Alexis Demers and Elizabeth Langevin, daughter of Joseph Langevin and Philomene Lagesse were married at Sacred Heart Church on Saturday, Aug. 14th, 1910
Sacred Heart Church was the second Catholic Church to be built in Southbridge in an area described as The Flats.

Now that he had remarried, Alexis went once again by train to Montreal to bring his son Eugene home at last. Elizabeth loved the young boy from the moment she set eyes on his cheerful, dimpled face. One year later, on August 25th 1911, Theodore Edouard was born, and two years after that came Roland.

Alexis was working at the American Optical Company as an engineer in charge of the boilers that powered that great enterprise. With encouragement from Elizabeth, they had saved enough to build a house.

The family moved to 87 Cliff Street in a house that they built on land purchased from Edouard. The house was a three-decker.

The streets of Globe Village and the Flats, two predominantly French neighborhoods, were lined with these three-deckers, a style that was responsible in part for the prosperity of the French who came to New England. One floor was for the owners and the other two were rented to relatives. Bank loans were soon paid off.

But all was not well with the family, for little Roland didn't seem to thrive and at the age of two, he became gravely ill and died. A photographer was called to take a final photograph. His mother, grief-stricken felt that she had been partly responsible. Fearing that raw milk contained bacteria, she had been feeding him boiled milk. Her theory was that it lacked nutrients. He had died of rickets.

Her depression increased by the day and taking care of little Teddy and Eugene became more difficult.

One morning, after sending Eugene off to school, she left the younger child with a neighbor saying that she'd return soon. In desperation she walked to the River Street Bridge that overlooked the Quinebaug River. She stood there for a long time, but she returned home when she felt a familiar stirring. She was pregnant once again. The new baby would also be named Roland. Elizabeth was forty-three when he was born.

CHAPTER 4
RHEA GERVAIS

Rhea was the first of the three Gervais sisters to marry. Her first choice for a husband was Michael Gregoire, the only blue-eyed brother of the four, but in 1913 he joined the cavalry in hopes of meeting General John Pershing.

Michael's dream wasn't realized and instead, he marched off to battle with over a million other young men when war with Germany was declared in 1917. After the war, he returned an invalid. He'd been gassed in the trenches.

His brothers, Joe, Romeo and Ovila were olive-skinned with piercing black eyes softened by ready smiles. They were all athletic and enjoyed wrestling, gymnastics and above all, sulky racing. All three worked at the American Optical Company.

The Gregoire family had come to Southbridge when Ovila was seven, just after he'd completed second grade in Canada. That was the end of his formal education.

Both families lived in Globe Village on Pleasant Street and, as a young man, Ovila often walked along with Rhea when she was on her way to work at Ames Worsted. He would walk her over the footbridge that crossed the Quinebaug River right to the door of the mill, and then would continue to his job at the American Optical Company.

She enjoyed his conversation for he was an avid storyteller and she found herself with tears of laughter on some of their walks. He remembered stories from his childhood in Quebec where the people held many superstitions. He told her of a stormy winter night when a lantern floating in air danced before a doctor's carriage as he was going to the bedside of a dying man. His driver, terrified at the apparition, raised his gun. The doctor shouted, "Don't shoot it, it's a good lantern sent by God!" Little did he know that Rhea, religious and superstitious herself, believed some of those stories that he found to be so amusing.

He was born in Joliette, a small town northeast of Montreal, the son of Joseph Gregoire and Caroline Boucher, daughter of Francois and Emelie Robert.

Ovila and Rhea were married on August 31st, 1914.

She became pregnant immediately and enjoyed her life as a housewife. She had four children in rapid succession. Sixteen years after having her first child, there would be a fifth child, Lucia, whom they called Lucy. Born in 1931, she was named after her godmother, Lucia Fisette, Rhea's youngest sister.

Estelle, the eldest, was born on May 31st, 1915 and soon baptized in the new Notre Dame Church on the day that the bells were blessed. The church, built of white marble held its own secret. The marble was purchased from a quarry that had made headstones for the dead of World War 1, but they'd prepared too many. The surplus stones were sold to the parish at a bargain price with enough to build the exquisite church and the rectory.

The Gregoire family had a large tenement in Globe Village on Pleasant Street, and Rhea, who enjoyed cooking and baking, would entertain relatives who came from Quebec and stayed for days on end. It was a joyous time for the families.

On Saturdays, her baking day, she'd awaken and after feeding her family, she'd bake ten pies and several loaves of bread. It was also the day when she'd make a huge pot of baked beans after soaking the beans overnight. She made brown bread, and the smell of molasses added to the aromas that filled the kitchen.

She made all the children's clothes, did knitting, crocheting and tailoring. She even sewed a cape of red velvet trimmed with rabbit fur for her statue of Jesus of Prague.

"Notice his eyes," she would tell the children. He follows you all over the room. Always do the right thing."

She once told them the story of the time that Aunt Lucia was angry with St. Anthony who had failed to help her to find her scissors so she buried his statue in the backyard. After a few days, she regretted her action and dug up the statue. It had turned green. She realized the error of her ways and went to confession.

Ovila was a steamfitter at the AO and brought home a respectable salary. An amateur wrestler, he entertained the children by teaching them wrestling moves. He also was a sulky racer and would take them to the racetrack to watch him compete in races. Rhea beamed at her muscular, agile husband. Like the women before her in Canada, it was she who taught him to read beyond his two years of schooling. When the busy household settled down and the children were asleep, the pair had quiet evenings drinking tea from big white mugs and eating her famous 'crybaby cookies' made of molasses. They would discuss the news of the day after reading the Southbridge Evening News and the Worcester Gazette. They had both voted for the Catholic candidate, Alfred Smith, but were finally pleased when the popular candidate, Herbert Hoover was elected in a landslide.

"This Hoover is quite a guy. Imagine, he was a poor farm boy from Iowa. Sounds like me."

Rhea nodded and looked down at her crocheting. She knew her husband liked stories about self-made men, but Hoover had also received scholarships to college. Ovila felt he'd accomplished something himself by getting a job at the American Optical Company. His wages were enough to support their family. His wife never would have to work.

Rhea's younger sisters, Lucia and Nettie were enjoying the fast pace of the flapper era and shocking their older relatives with their bobbed hair, short dresses and slang. It was an optimistic time, but storm clouds were gathering.

Ten-year-old Estelle loved her aunties who lived nearby with their mother, *Memere* Gervais. *Memere* had kicked out her husband in a very unusual move for a Victorian woman. Though he was handsome and charming, he didn't pay his bills and he spent a lot of time in the barroom. She didn't find it attractive when he came home slurring his words. She had even seen him relieving himself in the street.

Enough was enough and out he went. He moved to a little cabin down the street where he enjoyed talking to passersby, smoking his pipe and working as little as possible.

Memere was rid of the aggravation, but that meant that she had to go back to the mill, a small price to pay for a peaceful home.

Estelle would run over to their house at every opportunity. Watching the aunties apply makeup, she would beg them to teach her the latest dance steps and songs. The all-female home was a happy one.

Later, Aunt Lucia married Bill Fisette who owned a barbershop, a house and a small convenience store in Fiskdale, just west of Southbridge. Nettie moved to Springfield, Massachusetts and opened a beauty salon. She loved the hustle and bustle of the city and the sound of the trolleys outside her second floor window. She never married.

Uncle Joe, Rhea's brother, was now the only one who lived close to Rhea. He was a supervisor at the AO and a prosperous one. He owned a Victorian house on the corner of Pine and Marcy. Eva was his beautiful, redheaded wife who loved the color purple. Uncle Joe indulged her purchase of large purple hats adorned with feathers, proud to have her on his arm every Sunday as they walked to Notre Dame Church and down the aisle, his little peacock by his side.

Three years after her daughters moved away, Rhea's mother, *Memere* Gervais, just fifty- two years of age, died of a stroke while unlocking her door after work one day. The whole family was devastated by the loss of their wonderful *memere*.

Some weeks after the funeral, while Rhea was at the clothesline hanging out laundry, she heard the faint sound of rapping at the front door. She walked around the side of the house to see who was there. A couple of men stood there whom she didn't recognize.

The taller man spoke, his hat in his hand. "Sorry, Mrs. Gregoire, but your husband has had an accident. We've come to take you to the hospital. We're quite sure he'll pull through, but he looks bad right now."

Rhea ran into the house, removed her apron and grabbed her hat. The men had a company car and the hospital was a short distance away. When she entered the hospital room, there was her Ovila completely wrapped in bandages.

She found that he'd been injured when a huge steam pipe burst. He was burnt and his left arm was crushed under the pipe. That side of his body was badly injured. Though the burns were not severe, his muscles were destroyed from the length of his arm and down his left side.

The company doctor provided medical help that exacerbated the damage to his nerves. In addition to having a limp, his arm was useless.

From the day of his release from the hospital, Rhea would button his shirt, cut his meat, and carry the heavy kerosene can upstairs from the cellar to their second floor tenement, to fuel the oil heater.

That required two hands

There was no compensation except for the guarantee of a job. After his long recuperation, the AO hired him as a messenger boy.

The local tavern was a gathering place for men after work. No neighborhood was without one. Instead of going home after work, each man with his own sorrows walked through the door of the barroom and stayed longer than he'd planned. Ovila was no exception. Estelle often had the sorry job of going after him. "Come on, Pa. You've had enough. Mama is really mad at you and so am I." The men in the bar watched the spectacle of this lovely young lady tugging at her father's arm. Lifting their heads from their brew for a moment, with smiles on their faces they'd help her along. "Go on, Greg. The kid wants you to go home. See you tomorrow."

Like his brother, Joe Gregoire, all it took was two beers and he was drunk. That's when the storytelling would start. Ovila was the life of the party.

When she'd finally gotten him out the door, she'd walk ahead of him refusing to speak. By the time he'd crossed the River Street Bridge and walked to Pleasant Street, she was already seated at the table eating supper.

After seventeen years as a homemaker, Rhea, without the help of her dear mother and with a handicapped husband, chose to return to the Hamilton Woolen Company where she had worked as a weaver from the age of twelve until her marriage.

The family moved to Pine St. to be near her brother Joe.

"Why don't you come to the AO? I'm sure I can find something for you," Joe suggested, but Rhea preferred weaving.

"I understand the looms, and I like to be busy with my hands. I don't even mind the noise. It surrounds me with a rhythm and leaves me with my thoughts. I could run those looms in my sleep."

When Lucy was born in 1931, Rhea stayed home for three years.

Estelle and Rene had to leave school to support the family. They were both given jobs at the American Optical Company.

Lauretta and Claire were still in grammar school.

When Estelle married Ted Demers in 1934, Rhea went back to work and left little Lucy with her father, Ovila, who no longer worked. At the age of six, Lucy started school. Notre Dame *Academie Brochu* was right across the street from their home.

Rhea had a Spitz, a little black dog named Hustle, who knew just what time she'd be climbing the long hill home after work. He'd run to greet her and taking her gloves or lunch bag in his mouth he would prance beside her, his proud tail curled in a perfect O.

CHAPTER 5
THE DEMERS BROTHERS

Jean Baptiste and Edouard continued to prosper, but Alexis resisted enterprise. He had a silent nature and preferred to isolate himself. This was even more obvious from the time of the death of his first wife, Joanna, and later, that of his young son Roland, born to Elizabeth. After work, he found peace working in his garden, raising rabbits and bandy hens, and maintaining their property. He had one favorite hen named Celia who would wait for him at the door of the pen every morning knowing that he'd take her in the house and feed her bits of bread and bacon.

Elizabeth and Alexis took pride in their home. The front halls could only be used on Sundays and holidays to prevent wear and tear. The grounds were nicely landscaped with a lawn swing on the west side for all the occupants of the house to enjoy.

Lizzie, Alexis' pet name for Elizabeth, was the manager. She paid bills, collected rents and saved money.

The Wedding- 1912

Edouard had chosen a wife. Lydia was the only child of a Putnam attorney. She was as tall as Edouard and regal in appearance. She dressed in the latest fashion and her marceled hair was always perfect. Her husband doted on her and liked to see her wearing his gifts of jewelry.

He had purchased a ten-room house on Charlton Street next to his bakery. By the time of their marriage, it would be completely furnished and ready for her.

The wedding banns were announced for three Sundays and the marriage took place the following Saturday on a beautiful spring morning. A few friends and close family members from both sides were invited to the nuptial mass at Notre Dame Church. In addition to the bride and groom, the wedding party included Lydia's father and the groom's brothers, Jean Baptiste and Alexis.

The elegant bride wore a dress of Brandenberg lace with a high waist, full-length sleeves that tightened at the forearm, and a high ruff collar. Her veil fell to her shoulders from a cap of pearl beads that hugged her head. The groom wore a custom-made dark suit.

At the end of the mass, Edouard announced, "Please join us at our new home for some light refreshment."

The women couldn't wait to see the interior. The house was decorated in a dark but tasteful style. From the large front hall, one entered the parlor. The walls were papered in repetitive designs of birds and flowers and oriental rugs lay on dark hardwood floors. Tiffany lamps gave a soft light. The guests were led to button-back settees upholstered in burgundy velour, and to silk covered chairs.

Elizabeth, seated beside Alexis whispered, "My my." There was no more to say.

Introductions were made and the church organist played a few songs on the piano. Then, Edouard announced that refreshments would be served.

In the dining room, the housekeeper poured from a sterling silver tea set. Cucumber and watercress sandwiches were served from a pair of three -tiered ormolu stands of porcelain trimmed with gold. Between them, the crystal cake stand held a fruitcake with white frosting in scrolled designs. Small favors attached to ribbons had been baked inside. A coin promising wealth was most favored, and no one was surprised when Jean Baptiste was the lucky recipient.

A photographer was on hand to take photos of the gathering and, soon after, the guests were handed their coats. It would be their only visit to the couple's home.

In the future, Edouard attended family functions alone.

Jean Baptiste

Marriage was not on Jean Baptiste's mind. After founding the bank, he invested heavily in stocks. Never had he expected the stock market crash and bank failures that would occur in 1929.

Devastated after the bank closures he met Edouard in his office at the bakery. He ranted. "Do you know that Hoover has given the Germans a moratorium on paying reparations to France and England? Because of that, those two countries need handouts from us."

Edouard tried to calm him. "Perhaps you read too many newspapers. Times are bad but they certainly will improve. Southbridge is still a solvent town. Start over here. If anyone can do it, you can."

"Newspapers? You know what they call them now? Hoover blankets. That's all the poor have to cover themselves with." Edouard's attempts at diversion did not work as Jean Baptiste continued his diatribe against President Hoover. "Where is our popular president now? He is a dunce! Every decision he has made has been yet another way to destroy this economy. He sent thousands of Mexicans back to Mexico thinking they were taking American jobs. He put tariffs on foreign goods, and in retaliation the foreign countries have put tariffs on American goods so we aren't selling abroad; he won't help his own people because he doesn't believe that by failing to pour money into the economy, he has caused the depression to become worldwide. Worst of all, our own people are starving."

Edouard replied, " Look around you. The people in our town are not starving. Yes, they've lost their savings, but the Wells family has guaranteed that at least one member from each family will be guaranteed a job until this crisis is over."

The need for eyeglasses continued. The American Optical would survive, which meant the survival of Southbridge.

As the weeks went by, Edouard worried as he saw his oldest brother sink further into his own negative thoughts. He feared that, like some who had lost their fortunes, his brother would commit suicide.

When Jean Baptiste mentioned opportunities in California, his younger brother Edouard jumped at the chance to come to his aid.

"I have money. You know that my bank was under my mattress. I can help you to get started in a new business. How much will you need?" Edouard offered. After all, it was his JB who had led the family here to Massachusetts.

Within weeks, Jean Baptiste was on a train to California. He sent several postcards reporting what he'd seen on his trip.

"There are hobos everywhere. They jump the train at every stop. These are young men with harried faces. They are thin and hungry looking. The railroad detectives chase them away with sticks. They are carrying almost nothing. That could be me if it hadn't been for your help. I have the look of a gentleman, but now I know that the difference between those men and me is just a suit. God bless you, dear brother. JB"

Another card read,

"Passing through in the dark I see fires with crowds of men around them. They have blankets over their shoulders and the flames cast shadows on their wizened faces. These groups of men are everywhere along the tracks. What has happened to our country? JB"

Edouard didn't hear much more after Jean Baptiste reached California. There were a few letters about possible jobs and the poverty of Mexicans. He wrote, "Mexicans are being sent back to Mexico by the hundreds of thousands. I am doing a lot of walking and applying for the few jobs there are. I even tried the National Biscuit Company; I think I'll get something soon.

Have you read about the Okies? They have set up shacks here all over the city. So dear brother, it's me, the Okies and the Mexicans and we're all having a hard time. I ask myself 'why did I come here?' The answer is shame."

A few months later, Edouard received a telegram that his brother had suffered a heart attack.

He and Lydia made the long trip to Los Angeles by train, but by the time they had reached the hospital, Jean Baptiste was dead. They found that he'd been living in a single room with just a bed with a lumpy spring mattress and a worn coverlet. Beside it was a table that was covered with clippings of classified ads. On each, he'd written the date on which he'd applied and crossed them out with a black x. In a jar was his final money, $7.42.

CHAPTER 6
A NEW GENERATION

E douard had no children, but he had plans for his godson, Teddy, who was born in 1911. He saw himself in that young man. Alexis was the boy's father but he was nothing like him.

At the age of eleven Teddy had a paper route with over sixty customers. He kept all his accounts in his head and never missed a day even in winter, when he had to trudge through deep snow. He charmed his women customers and sweetly asked them if they had any soap coupons. He managed to accumulate enough of them to get a wagon. With the wagon, he increased the number of papers that he could carry and earned enough to buy himself a sled, a Flexible Flyer.

Edouard wanted Teddy to attend high school. His goal was to send both nephews to college. It was time for the Demers family to get some education. Teddy had his own plans. He preferred to work. Edouard didn't discourage him. The boy had a decent hand, was a reader and knew sums. That would do. He soon accepted a job in uncle's bakery, but working inside didn't suit him. He was thrilled with his first bread truck with Par X Bakery written on the side. One of twenty drivers, his route was just over the state line into Connecticut, and included the towns of Woodstock, Eastford and Ashford.

His customers, mostly farmers, lived far apart except for those around the town common. There, grand homes from the eighteenth and nineteenth centuries housed the lawyers, the country doctor, the judge, and the most prosperous businessmen. A simple church, its steeple rising high into the sky, reflected the aspirations of the inhabitants, both worldly and spiritually.

The most prosperous village was Woodstock Hill with grand homes, the Academy, and Roseland Cottage, a humbly named estate. It was built by a wealthy New York stockbroker. A number of presidents were entertained there during Victorian 4th of July celebrations.

Teddy worked six days a week. His day would start at 7:00 a.m. and end at 11:00 p.m. or midnight, depending on the weather and flat tires. Sometimes he'd have to rely on a farmer and his horse to pull the truck out of a ditch after he'd skidded in the snow.

His customers provided him with an active social life. They sometimes disagreed with Ted politically, for this was Yankee country and they were all Republicans. They were also Protestants. Conversation came with a good meal and homemade pie. His customers appreciated the small favors he would do for them like picking up a prescription or bringing newspapers and bullets.

Over the years he learned which house had a dog to watch out for. Then there were geese and billygoats that aimed for the rear. The geese gave warnings, but the goats did not. He also knew that some housewives were very lonely and he had to make a quick getaway when they had a certain look in their eyes. He learned the locations of clotheslines by walking into one occasionally in the dark.

At the end of his route he'd leave bread and doughnuts stacked on the porch, in an old ice chest, in the mailbox or in a box near the door while the family slept inside.

At the bakery on Charlton Street, Edouard ranked his bread deliverymen according to how many loaves they sold and entered their names on a board for all to see.

Each week, Teddy's name was at the top of the chart.

Thursday night was his early night. It was payday in Southbridge and Main St. came to life. It was a time for shopping and enjoyment. He enjoyed dances, vaudeville, wrestling matches, the fights, and the big bands that came to Southbridge. Meeting girls was his goal and there were usually a few waiting for him at the dances.

His older brother, Gene, now a prosperous young man at the AO, would sometimes let him use his open touring car and borrow his raccoon coat. Then, Teddy was really King of the Hill.

CHAPTER 7

ESTELLE

After one year of high school, Estelle went to work at the American Optical Company to help her family. She never did live the life of her flapper aunts in the early twenties, for the Great Depression followed those halcyon days. For three summers she had lived with Aunt Lucia and Uncle Bill in Fiskdale, where she was a companion to Gloria, their only child, who was ten years younger than she.

They loved Estelle like a daughter. Aunt Lucia was busy teaching piano and playing the organ at church. Uncle Bill was a barber and had a small general store attached to the house. Gloria had elocution lessons and tap lessons each week. She was their Shirley Temple.

Estelle and her family were hard hit by the loss of Ovila's earning power after his accident. His salary as a messenger boy was much less than that of a steamfitter. In spite of those changes, she felt very grownup going off to work every day and she made new friends.

One young woman, her friend, Mary, was Italian and often invited her to her home where her Sicilian mother cooked wonderful dishes and called her Stella. The mother couldn't speak English, but her food spoke love and warmth.

Both Estelle and Mary worked in a polishing room where they polished lenses.

Estelle's tall, sophisticated looks weren't lost on the men. Even George Wells, the owner of the AO, would pause before her bench for a bit of conversation. It was a time of wolf whistles and flirting. Her outstanding features were her large blue eyes and her long dark hair which she wore in a chignon.

"Hey, Loretta Young, look this way," was a comment she often heard from would-be suitors.

Her friend Lorraine introduced her to her cousin, Teddy. He was handsome and ambitious with a ready smile. He was twenty and she was sixteen.

He charmed her parents and she was allowed to go out with him, but not to dances. Their dates were walks, often to ice cream parlors, movies, and canoeing. The latter was not a sport for her. She would wear her best summer dress, a big hat and high heels. Teddy would carry her to the canoe and he would paddle. She was allowed to date just once a week and she was expected to go right home from work.

Leaving the AO, at the end of the day, Estelle would look with envy at the young women who went on to play tennis and who got to keep their earnings to spend on clothes and fun.

Ted and Estelle married in 1934, three years after they met. By that time, he owned 81 Cliff Street. The four tenements were rented to relatives. He and Estelle moved into his parents' house on the first floor of 87 Cliff Street.

Their home was completely furnished before they moved in. Teddy was a saver and they had fun setting up housekeeping and paying cash for everything.

"If you don't have the money for it, don't buy it," was his lifelong motto.

They went to New York City by train on their honeymoon, and stayed at the Taft Hotel. They loved the Automat and spotting Joe Louis and Jack Dempsey at the Brass Rail Restaurant on 7th Avenue and 49th Street. It was the place to see and be seen. It was their first trip to the Big Apple. Estelle, who loved high heels learned that they weren't the best for walking but for her, fashion came first, at least for a couple of days.

When they returned to Southbridge and opened the door to their new home, Teddy carried her over the threshold. As he put her down in the kitchen with the shiny inlaid linoleum floor and the new cream- colored Glenwood Range he said, "You'll never have to work again, Estelle," She wasn't sure that was such a good idea. She would miss her friends, but he was her husband after all. Hers was not a questioning nature and from that point on Teddy made all the decisions.

Their first child, a girl, was born in October of 1935. She was named Patricia Claire Demers.

She was the first grandchild on both sides and was surrounded by grandparents, aunts, uncles, cousins, and a doting godmother and godfather, Aunt Claire and Uncle Roland.

Estelle didn't have time to miss her job or her friends. She had three children in five years. Kenneth was born in 1937 and Donald in 1940.

In 1945, the young family had a very special Christmas gift! Teddy had bought a summerhouse in Woodstock, Connecticut. It was a 19th century house surrounded by farms, fields, and forests. Pond Factory was nearby for swimming.

The former owners would rent from Ted until June and the day after school closed, the family would be off to Woodstock for the whole summer!

CHAPTER 8
A YEAR OF CHANGES-1949

A fourth child joined the family. Paulette was born on January 4th, 1949, much to the excitement of her older sister, Patty, who was thirteen. By that time, Ted's business had expanded in Connecticut and it made sense for the family to live in Woodstock permanently.

Ted had an addition put on the house, once again hoping to surprise his family before their move in June. Estelle wasn't consulted about the design but after protesting she was allowed to select the furnishings and to decorate the new rooms.

Uncle Edouard had made the move to Woodstock, Connecticut several years earlier. He had purchased a large yellow house on Woodstock Hill. A veranda wrapped around the house on two sides, and the driveway that led to a two-car garage was lined with cherry trees.

He learned from neighbors that his was a 'spite house' built by a man whose goal was to block his neighbor's view from across the street. The reason for the quarrel was unknown to Edouard.

The house had a sweeping view to the east and several acres of lawn that rolled down toward the new elementary school where he'd donated the furniture for the teachers' lounge in the new elementary school.

The new school opened in 1951, two years after the Demers family moved to North Woodstock. For the first two years, the boys, Kenneth and Donald, attended a one-room schoolhouse. Patty went to Woodstock Academy, a private school for which the town paid tuition.

In winter, Edouard sometimes invited the Demers children to go sledding on his hill. He brought out hot chocolate and the gum machine that he'd entertained them with for years. He sat on the large porch admiring the family. He often told Teddy, "If Lydia survives me, and I doubt that she will, for she is bedridden much of the time, you will be the one to inherit all that I have. Take good care of it."

It was his joy to mow his acres on his riding lawnmower. His wife never allowed him to enter the house in work clothes so it was his custom to change at the entrance where there was a large closet in the walk-in basement.

In addition to taking care of his property, he loved politics. He served on the Woodstock Board of Education, the democratic town committee and the board of finance. He encouraged his nephew, Teddy, to do the same.

It wasn't long before Teddy followed in his footsteps on the school board. He joined the volunteer firemen and coached Little League in the summer.

Ted's younger brother, Roland, moved to Woodstock Valley and opened a general store attached to the post office where he became postmaster. His charm wasn't lost on the residents who enjoyed coming for their mail each day. Together with his lovely wife, Little Irene, and their three children, they were favorites in the neighborhood.

Years earlier, Gene and Big Irene had moved to Sturbridge where she opened a bed and breakfast, and he continued to work at the American Optical Company. They had two children.

Edouard, who had no children, planned that his nephews would enjoy the fruits of his labor. His greatest indulgence was his car. Every two years he bought a Lincoln Continental. The year that he was going to trade in his pink Lincoln, Ted bought it from him for Estelle who was learning to drive.

Patty was the only family member who had dined at the home of Edouard and Lydia. Ted couldn't drive her to the dance one winter evening so he'd asked Uncle Edouard to take her as a special favor. Estelle hadn't gotten her license yet.

The day of the dance, Patty walked the short distance to Edouard's house from the Academy, and after supper, Edouard drove her to the dance and later picked her up and drove her home to Rawson Road.

"It was so dark in there, Mom," she said, "the only light was in the kitchen. Aunt Lydia got up from her bed to come to dinner. She sat at the table, but she didn't even talk to me. Uncle Edouard did all the talking. I changed my clothes in the next room, a bedroom where a lamp was turned on. Everything was perfect, like a hotel."

In September of 1955 when Patty was at college, she got a call from her father that Uncle Edouard was dead. After mowing his lawn, he dropped dead in the entrance to the walk-in basement. Lydia was in bed, as usual, but the housekeeper found him when he didn't come up for lunch.

The day of his funeral at Notre Dame Church in Southbridge, there was a huge crowd in attendance. There were family members, business owners, politicians… but one person was absent.

Lydia had dismissed her housekeeper, called a taxi and gone to the hairdresser's. The family had no further contact with her. A year later, she too was dead. Hers was a private funeral in Putnam.

After talking to his brother, Eugene (whose wife was referred to as 'Big Irene' because Roland's wife who was younger, was also Irene), Ted called Roland.

"Big Irene stopped at Uncle's house," he said. "You know she's good at looking after things. She told me that the lawyer and his wife were there a few days after Lydia's funeral. They were choosing furniture and having it put in a truck for themselves. I went to his office to see about the will. It seems that Aunt Lydia made some changes. You and I will each get a few thousand dollars. The bulk of the estate has gone to Aunt Lydia's church and to her family. I'm sorry."

Home from college for the weekend, Patty was shocked to hear the news. "Dad, you must contest it. Everyone knows it was meant to be yours." Teddy shrugged his shoulders. He shrugged them because he was French. He shrugged them because he was Catholic and believed in fate.

"Be happy with what you have." He always was.

In the sixties, many of the New England mills moved south. Their empty shells became discount shops, art studios, heritage sites, or were just plain abandoned and boarded up.

By that time, the families of the Little Canadas had largely dispersed. Like the Demers family who had moved to Sturbridge and Woodstock and then beyond, many of the children and grandchildren of the second great migration had college degrees and followed job opportunities as the United States became an information society.

Other migrants now took their place, coming from such diverse countries as Mexico, Vietnam, and from our own American possession, Puerto Rico.

Like the French, Irish, Italians, and Greeks that came before them, these newcomers would become the new Americans.

In Southbridge, Spanish can be heard on the streets instead of French. *Notre Dame Academie Brochu* is on the register of historic places, and the Little Canadas are now history. Massachusetts remains the state with the greatest number of French speakers in the nation.

Je me souviens.

Patrice Demers Kaneda
December 4, 2012

CPSIA information can be obtained at www.ICGtesting.com
Printed in the USA
BVOW03s1741140514

353505BV00008B/200/P